KRYPTO
The SUPERDOG ™

SUPERMAN CREATED BY
JERRY SIEGEL AND JOE SHUSTER
BY SPECIAL ARRANGEMENT WITH
THE JERRY SIEGEL FAMILY

STONE ARCH BOOKS
a capstone imprint

△△ STONE ARCH BOOKS™
Published in 2014
A Capstone Imprint
1710 Roe Crest Drive
North Mankato, MN 56003
www.capstonepub.com

Originally published by DC Comics in the U.S. in single magazine form as
Kryto The Superdog #6. Copyright © 2014 DC Comics. All Rights Reserved.

DC Comics
1700 Broadway, New York, NY 10019
A Warner Bros. Entertainment Company

No part of this publication may be reproduced in whole or in part, or stored in a retrieval
system, or transmitted in any form or by any means, electronic, mechanical, photocopying,
recording, or otherwise, without written permission.

Cataloging-in-Publication Data is available at the
Library of Congress website
ISBN: 978-1-4342-6472-5 (library binding)

Summary: Most dogs chase mail carriers, and Krypto is no exception! But why are he and
the Dog Star Patrol chasing a space mailman?

STONE ARCH BOOKS
Ashley C. Andersen Zantop Publisher
Michael Dahl Editorial Director
Donald Lemke & Sean Tulien Editors
Bob Lentz Art Director
Hilary Wacholz Designer

DC COMICS
Kristy Quinn Original U.S. Editor

Printed in China by Nordica.
1013 / CA21301918
092013   007744NORDS14

KRYPTO
The SUPERDOG ™

Houndin' the Mail Carrier!

JESSE LEON MCCANN......................................WRITER

MIN. S. KU ....PENCILLER

JEFF ALBRECHT...INKER

DAVE TANGUAY ....COLORIST

DAVE TANGUAY ....LETTERER

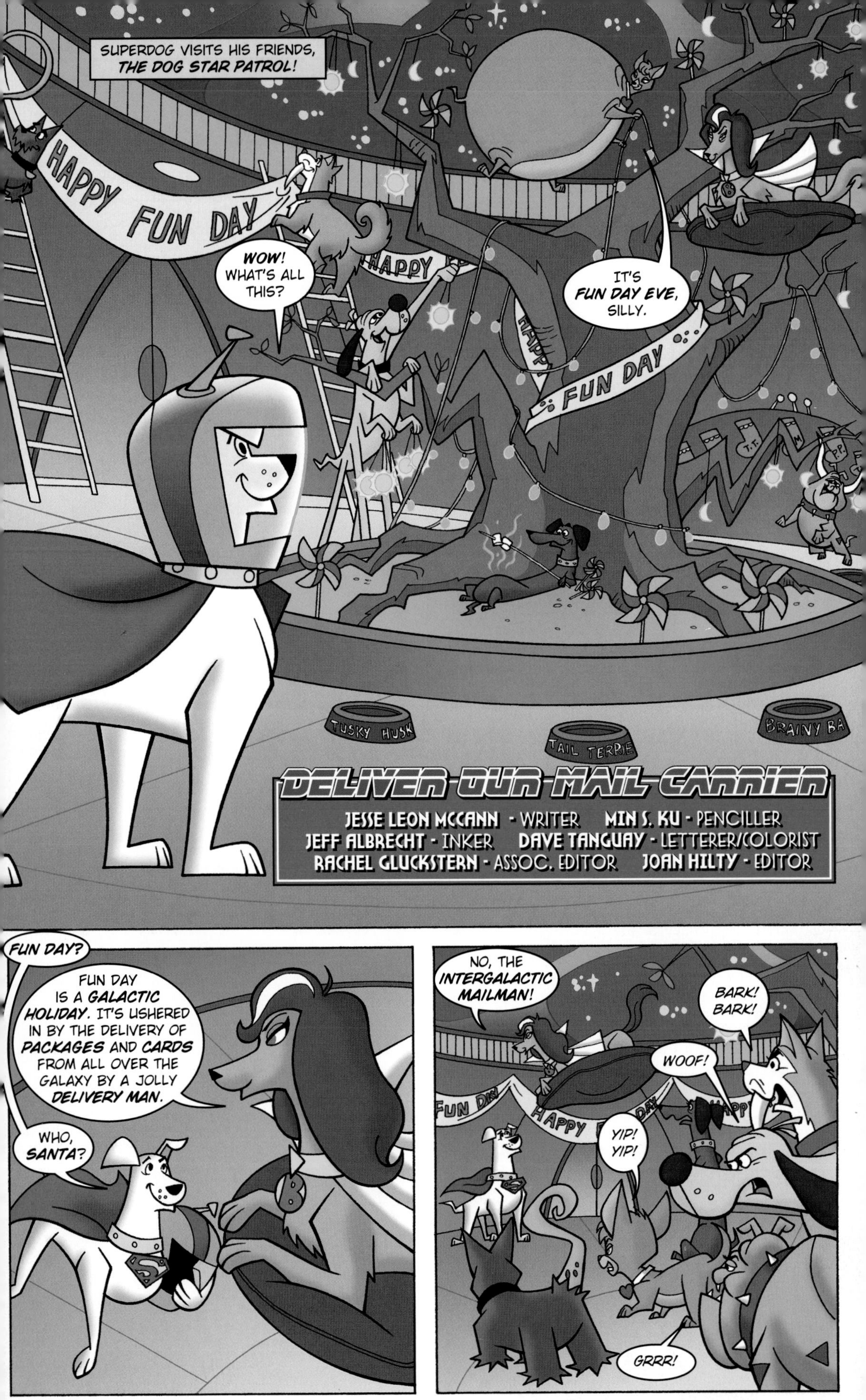
SUPERDOG VISITS HIS FRIENDS, THE DOG STAR PATROL!
HAPPY FUN DAY
WOW! WHAT'S ALL THIS?
IT'S FUN DAY EVE, SILLY.
HAPPY
FUN DAY
TUSKY HUSK
TAIL TERRIE
BRAINY BA
DELIVER OUR MAIL CARRIER
JESSE LEON MCCANN - WRITER MIN S. KU - PENCILLER
JEFF ALBRECHT - INKER DAVE TANGUAY - LETTERER/COLORIST
RACHEL GLUCKSTERN - ASSOC. EDITOR JOAN HILTY - EDITOR
FUN DAY?
FUN DAY IS A GALACTIC HOLIDAY. IT'S USHERED IN BY THE DELIVERY OF PACKAGES AND CARDS FROM ALL OVER THE GALAXY BY A JOLLY DELIVERY MAN.
WHO, SANTA?
NO, THE INTERGALACTIC MAILMAN!
BARK! BARK!
WOOF!
YIP! YIP!
GRRR!

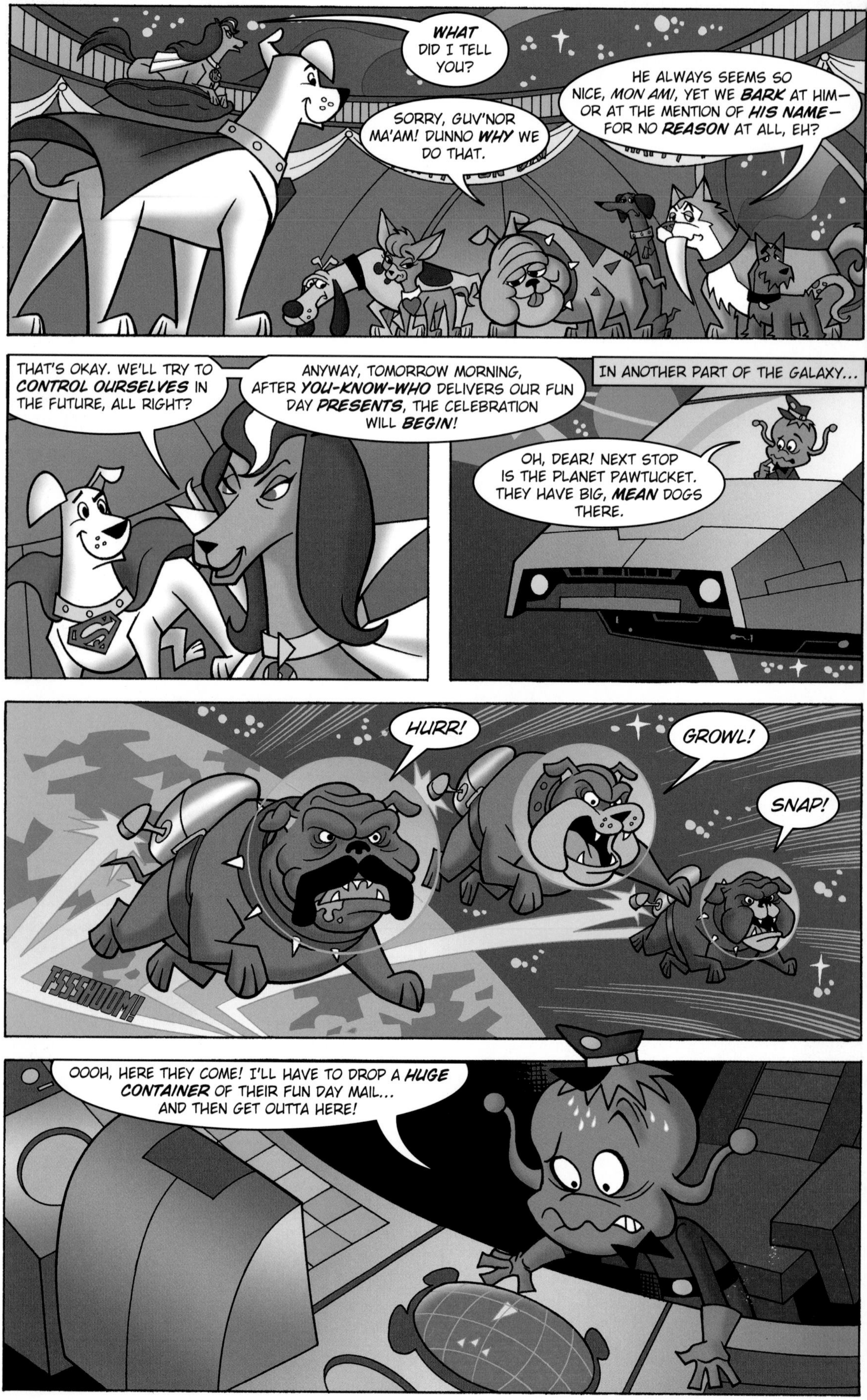
WHAT DID I TELL YOU?
SORRY, GUV'NOR MA'AM! DUNNO WHY WE DO THAT.
HE ALWAYS SEEMS SO NICE, MON AMI, YET WE BARK AT HIM—OR AT THE MENTION OF HIS NAME—FOR NO REASON AT ALL, EH?
THAT'S OKAY. WE'LL TRY TO CONTROL OURSELVES IN THE FUTURE, ALL RIGHT?
ANYWAY, TOMORROW MORNING, AFTER YOU-KNOW-WHO DELIVERS OUR FUN DAY PRESENTS, THE CELEBRATION WILL BEGIN!
IN ANOTHER PART OF THE GALAXY...
OH, DEAR! NEXT STOP IS THE PLANET PAWTUCKET. THEY HAVE BIG, MEAN DOGS THERE.
HURR!
GROWL!
SNAP!
FSSSHOOM!
OOOH, HERE THEY COME! I'LL HAVE TO DROP A HUGE CONTAINER OF THEIR FUN DAY MAIL... AND THEN GET OUTTA HERE!

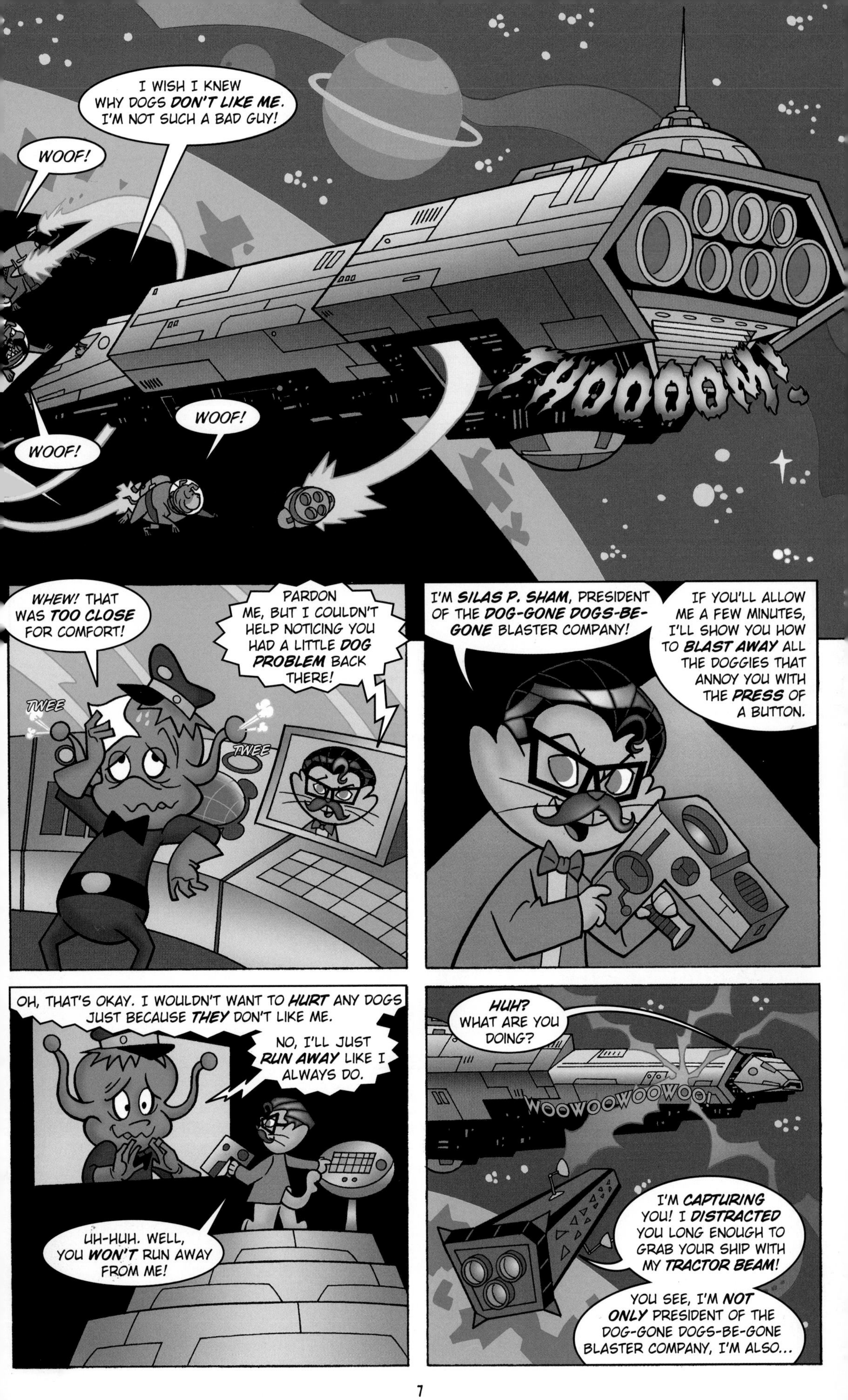
I WISH I KNEW WHY DOGS DON'T LIKE ME. I'M NOT SUCH A BAD GUY!
WOOF!
WOOF!
WOOF!
WHOOOOM!
WHEW! THAT WAS TOO CLOSE FOR COMFORT!
PARDON ME, BUT I COULDN'T HELP NOTICING YOU HAD A LITTLE DOG PROBLEM BACK THERE!
TWEE
TWEE
I'M SILAS P. SHAM, PRESIDENT OF THE DOG-GONE DOGS-BE-GONE BLASTER COMPANY!
IF YOU'LL ALLOW ME A FEW MINUTES, I'LL SHOW YOU HOW TO BLAST AWAY ALL THE DOGGIES THAT ANNOY YOU WITH THE PRESS OF A BUTTON.
OH, THAT'S OKAY. I WOULDN'T WANT TO HURT ANY DOGS JUST BECAUSE THEY DON'T LIKE ME.
NO, I'LL JUST RUN AWAY LIKE I ALWAYS DO.
UH-HUH. WELL, YOU WON'T RUN AWAY FROM ME!
HUH? WHAT ARE YOU DOING?
WOOWOOWOOWOO!
I'M CAPTURING YOU! I DISTRACTED YOU LONG ENOUGH TO GRAB YOUR SHIP WITH MY TRACTOR BEAM!
YOU SEE, I'M NOT ONLY PRESIDENT OF THE DOG-GONE DOGS-BE-GONE BLASTER COMPANY, I'M ALSO...

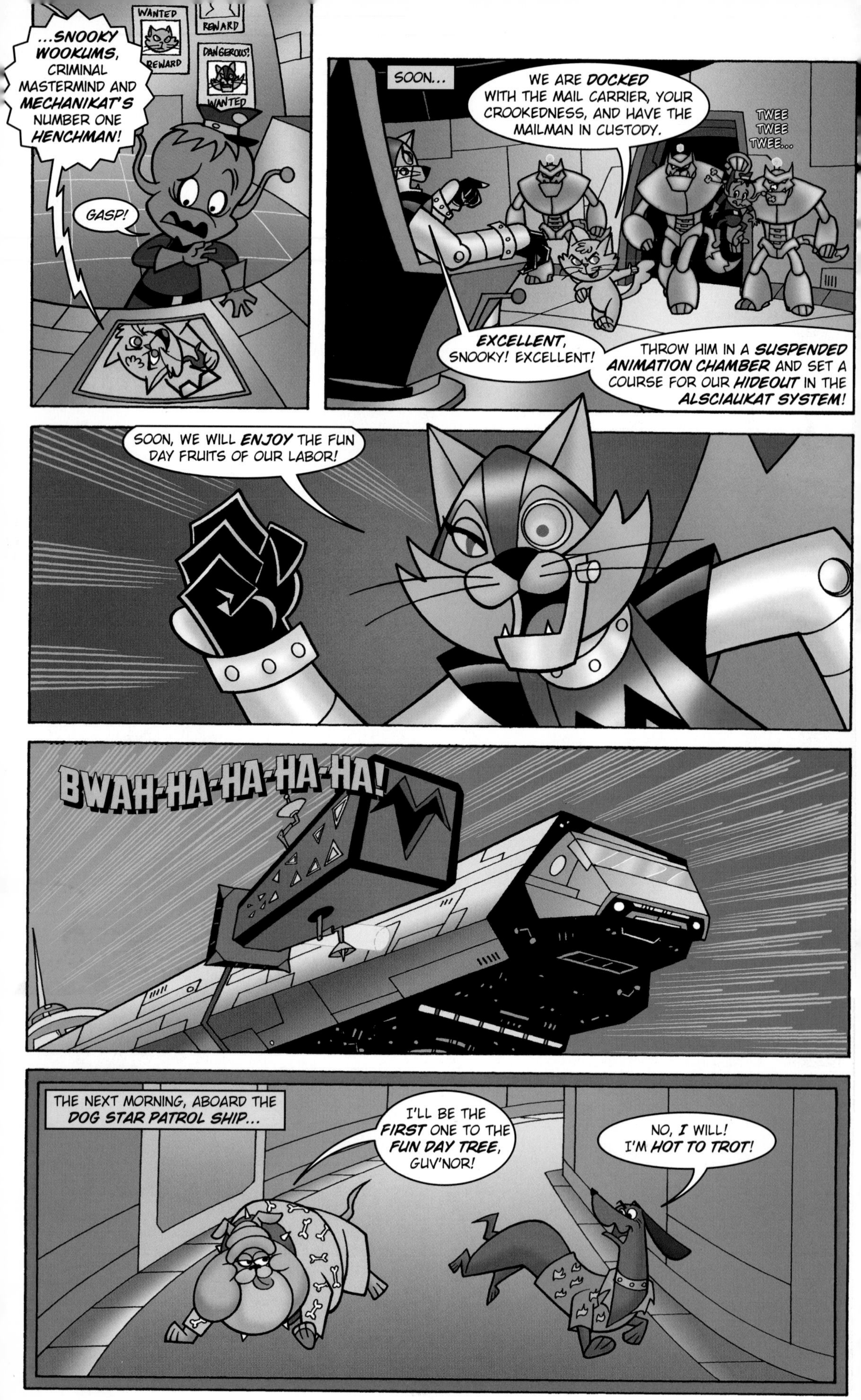
WANTED
REWARD
REWARD
DANGEROUS!
WANTED
...SNOOKY WOOKUMS, CRIMINAL MASTERMIND AND MECHANIKAT'S NUMBER ONE HENCHMAN!
GASP!
SOON...
WE ARE DOCKED WITH THE MAIL CARRIER, YOUR CROOKEDNESS, AND HAVE THE MAILMAN IN CUSTODY.
TWEE TWEE TWEE...
EXCELLENT, SNOOKY! EXCELLENT!
THROW HIM IN A SUSPENDED ANIMATION CHAMBER AND SET A COURSE FOR OUR HIDEOUT IN THE ALSCIAUKAT SYSTEM!
SOON, WE WILL ENJOY THE FUN DAY FRUITS OF OUR LABOR!
BWAH-HA-HA-HA-HA!
THE NEXT MORNING, ABOARD THE DOG STAR PATROL SHIP...
I'LL BE THE FIRST ONE TO THE FUN DAY TREE, GUV'NOR!
NO, I WILL! I'M HOT TO TROT!

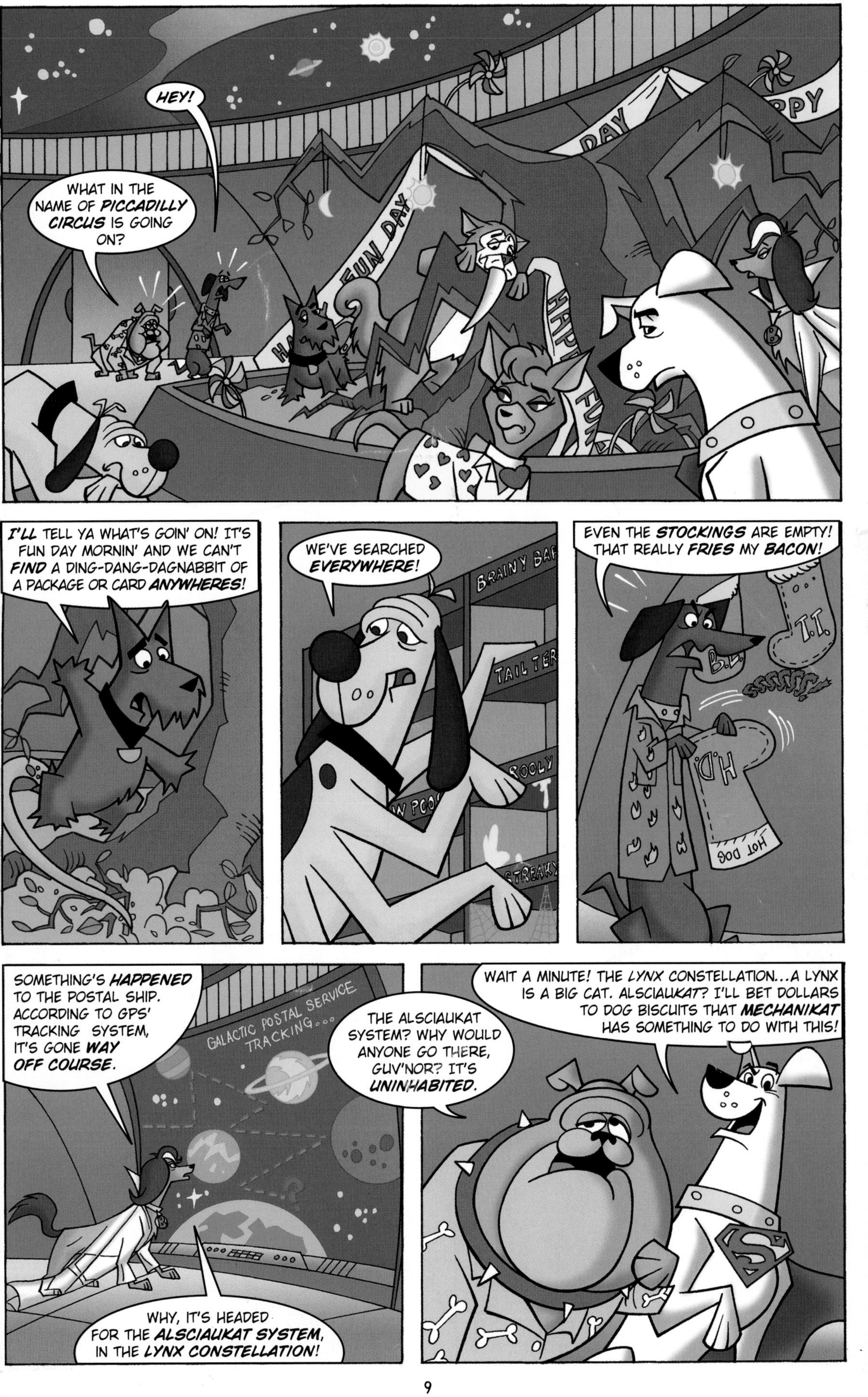

HEY!
WHAT IN THE NAME OF PICCADILLY CIRCUS IS GOING ON?
FUN DAY
I'LL TELL YA WHAT'S GOIN' ON! IT'S FUN DAY MORNIN' AND WE CAN'T FIND A DING-DANG-DAGNABBIT OF A PACKAGE OR CARD ANYWHERES!
WE'VE SEARCHED EVERYWHERE!
EVEN THE STOCKINGS ARE EMPTY! THAT REALLY FRIES MY BACON!
T.T.
HOT DOG
SOMETHING'S HAPPENED TO THE POSTAL SHIP. ACCORDING TO GPS' TRACKING SYSTEM, IT'S GONE WAY OFF COURSE.
GALACTIC POSTAL SERVICE TRACKING...
WHY, IT'S HEADED FOR THE ALSCIAUKAT SYSTEM, IN THE LYNX CONSTELLATION!
THE ALSCIAUKAT SYSTEM? WHY WOULD ANYONE GO THERE, GUV'NOR? IT'S UNINHABITED.
WAIT A MINUTE! THE LYNX CONSTELLATION...A LYNX IS A BIG CAT. ALSCIAUKAT? I'LL BET DOLLARS TO DOG BISCUITS THAT MECHANIKAT HAS SOMETHING TO DO WITH THIS!

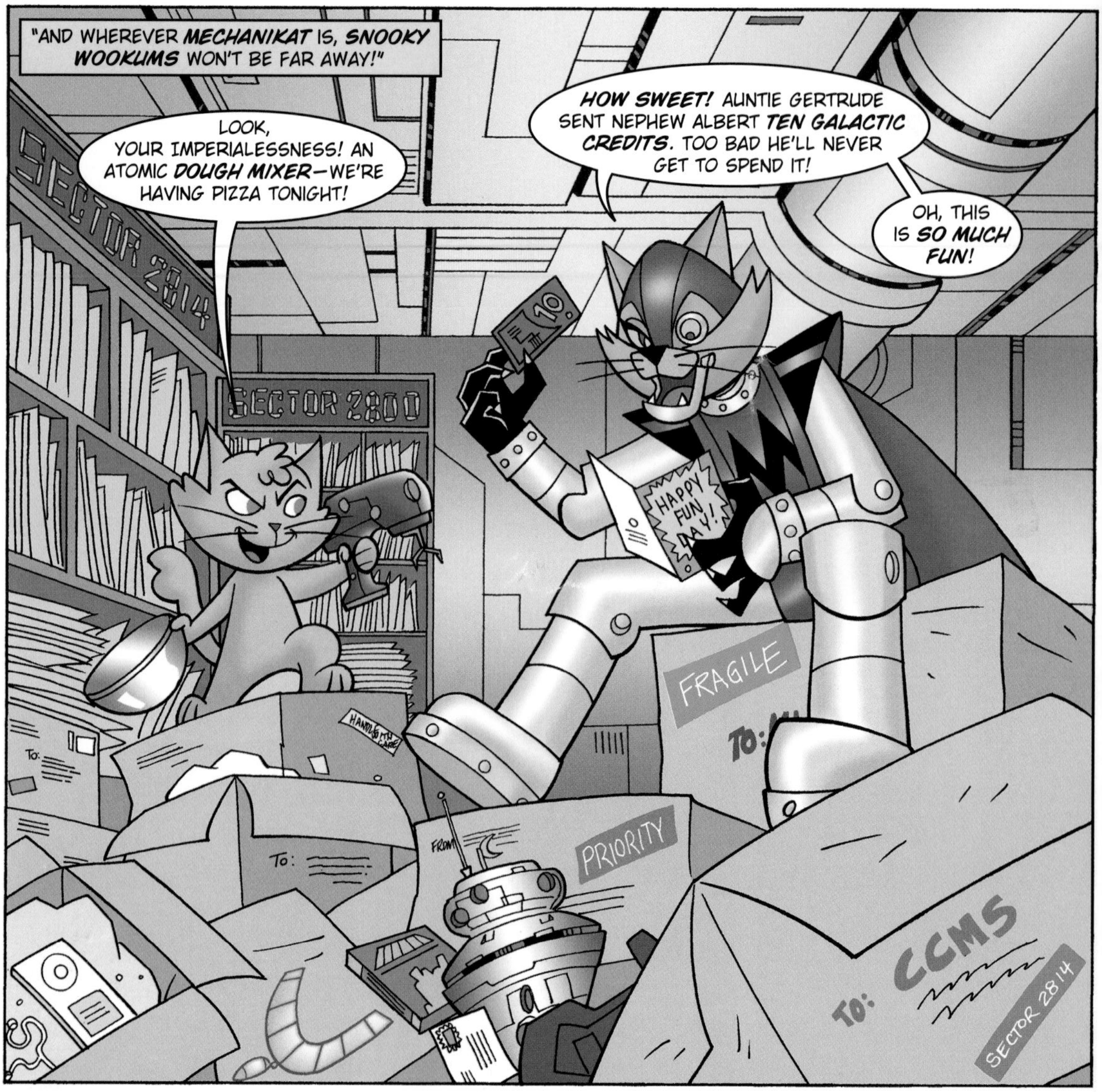
"AND WHEREVER MECHANIKAT IS, SNOOKY WOOKUMS WON'T BE FAR AWAY!"
LOOK, YOUR IMPERIALESSNESS! AN ATOMIC DOUGH MIXER—WE'RE HAVING PIZZA TONIGHT!
HOW SWEET! AUNTIE GERTRUDE SENT NEPHEW ALBERT TEN GALACTIC CREDITS. TOO BAD HE'LL NEVER GET TO SPEND IT!
OH, THIS IS SO MUCH FUN!
SECTOR 2814
SECTOR 2800
HAPPY FUN DAY!
FRAGILE
PRIORITY
TO: CCMS
SECTOR 2814

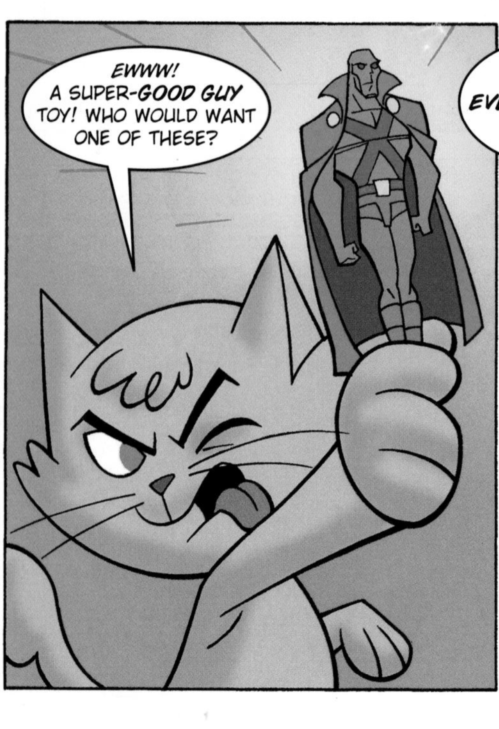
EWWW! A SUPER-GOOD GUY TOY! WHO WOULD WANT ONE OF THESE?

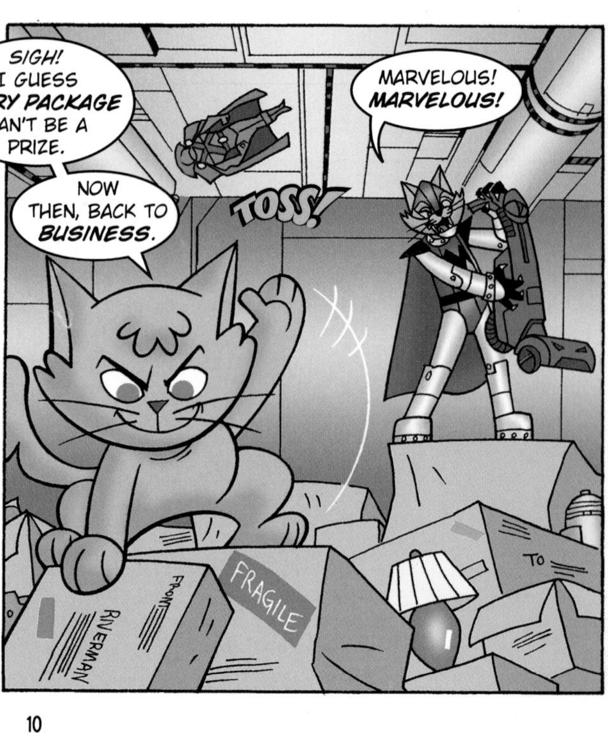
SIGH! I GUESS EVERY PACKAGE CAN'T BE A PRIZE.
NOW THEN, BACK TO BUSINESS.
MARVELOUS! MARVELOUS!
TOSS!
FRAGILE
FROM

To:
CRASH!
HOLD IT RIGHT THERE, YOU ***FELONIOUS FELINES!***
WHA-?
YOU PICKED THE ***WRONG HOLIDAY*** TO MESS WITH, BUSTER!
NOW YOU SHALL GET THE ***TOOTH***, THE ***WHOLE TOOTH*** AND ***NOTHING BUT*** THE TOOTH.
ENOUGH CHITCHAT! LET'S ***WRANGLE*** THESE CROOKED KITTIES!
TO: JESSE L. M.
TAIL TERRIER AND I WILL HANDLE THESE TWO. THE REST OF YOU RESCUE THE ***MAILMAN!***
YIP! YIP!
DOG STARS!
WOOF!
GRRR!
BARK! BARK!
OOPS.
ANYWAY... WE'LL BE ***GOING*** NOW, EH?
SORRY, SORRY.
DUNNO WHY WE DO THAT.
YEAH! IT'S TIME TO SAVE... ***THAT GUY!***
RIGHT-O! NOTHIN' CAN STOP US FROM RESCUIN' ***...HIM!***

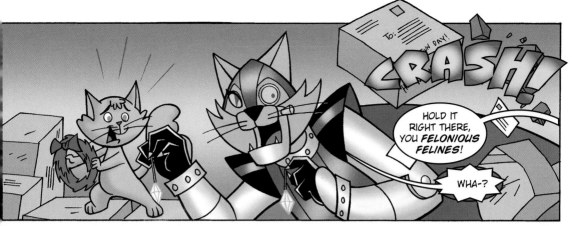

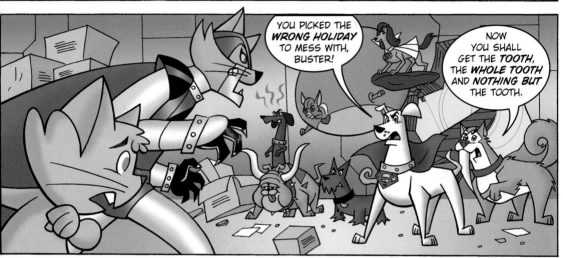

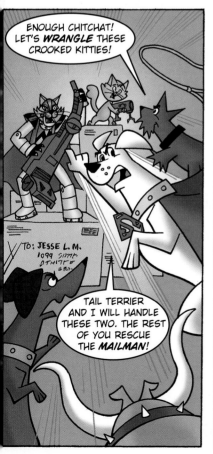

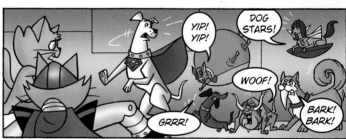

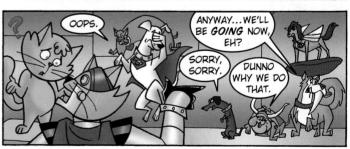

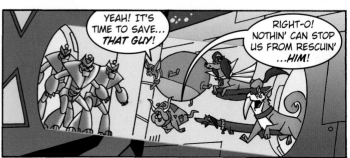

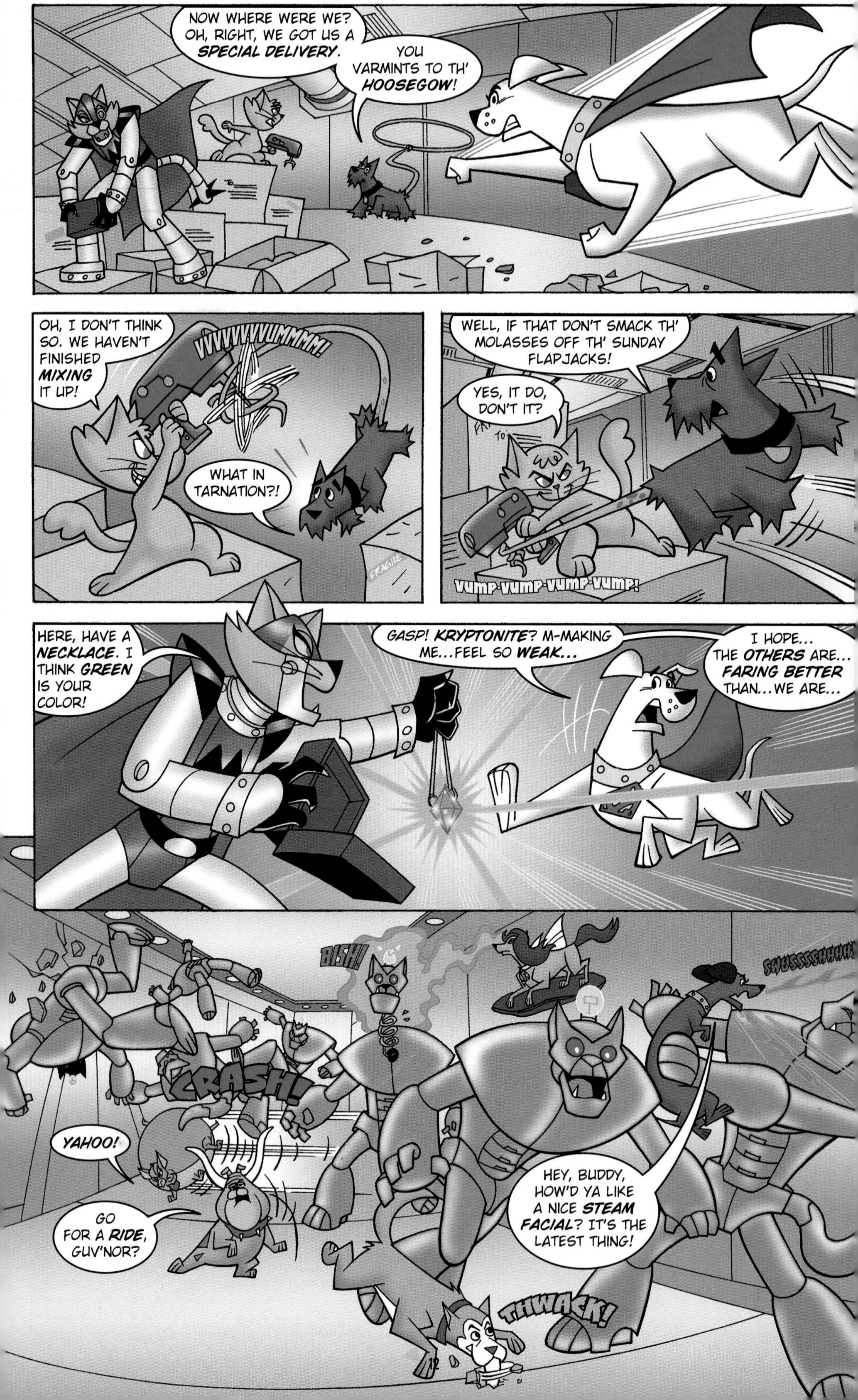
NOW WHERE WERE WE? OH, RIGHT, WE GOT US A SPECIAL DELIVERY.
YOU VARMINTS TO TH' HOOSEGOW!
OH, I DON'T THINK SO. WE HAVEN'T FINISHED MIXING IT UP!
VVVVVVVVUMMMM!
WHAT IN TARNATION?!
FRAGILE
WELL, IF THAT DON'T SMACK TH' MOLASSES OFF TH' SUNDAY FLAPJACKS!
YES, IT DO, DON'T IT?
VUMP-VUMP-VUMP-VUMP!
HERE, HAVE A NECKLACE. I THINK GREEN IS YOUR COLOR!
GASP! KRYPTONITE? M-MAKING ME...FEEL SO WEAK...
I HOPE... THE OTHERS ARE... FARING BETTER THAN... WE ARE...
BISH!
SWUSSSSHHHH!
CRASH!
YAHOO!
GO FOR A RIDE, GUV'NOR?
HEY, BUDDY, HOW'D YA LIKE A NICE STEAM FACIAL? IT'S THE LATEST THING!
THWACK!

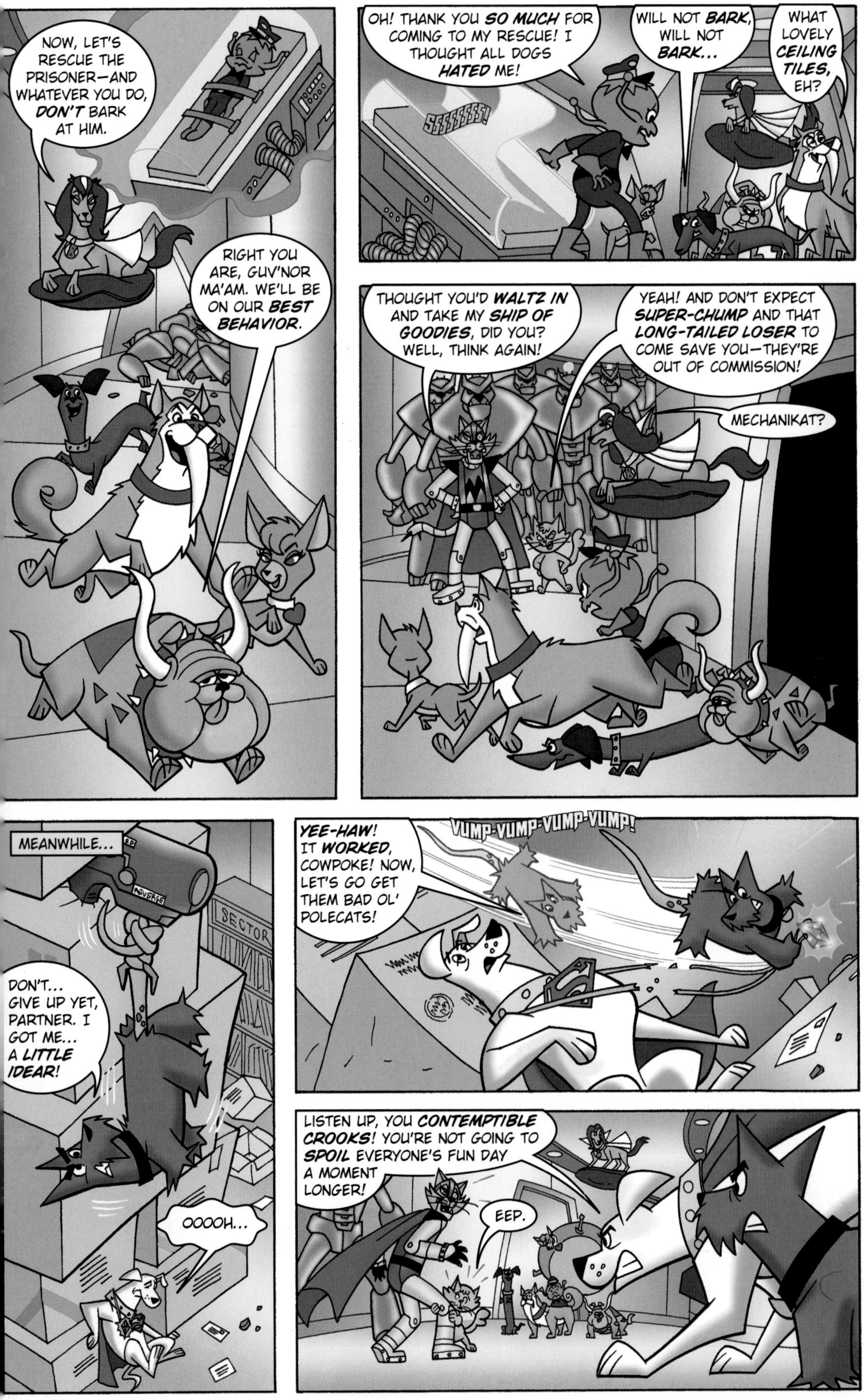
NOW, LET'S RESCUE THE PRISONER—AND WHATEVER YOU DO, DON'T BARK AT HIM.
RIGHT YOU ARE, GUV'NOR MA'AM. WE'LL BE ON OUR BEST BEHAVIOR.
OH! THANK YOU SO MUCH FOR COMING TO MY RESCUE! I THOUGHT ALL DOGS HATED ME!
SSSSSSSS!
WILL NOT BARK, WILL NOT BARK...
WHAT LOVELY CEILING TILES, EH?
THOUGHT YOU'D WALTZ IN AND TAKE MY SHIP OF GOODIES, DID YOU? WELL, THINK AGAIN!
YEAH! AND DON'T EXPECT SUPER-CHUMP AND THAT LONG-TAILED LOSER TO COME SAVE YOU—THEY'RE OUT OF COMMISSION!
MECHANIKAT?
MEANWHILE...
SECTOR
DON'T... GIVE UP YET, PARTNER. I GOT ME... A LITTLE IDEAR!
OOOOH...
VUMP-VUMP-VUMP-VUMP!
YEE-HAW! IT WORKED, COWPOKE! NOW, LET'S GO GET THEM BAD OL' POLECATS!
LISTEN UP, YOU CONTEMPTIBLE CROOKS! YOU'RE NOT GOING TO SPOIL EVERYONE'S FUN DAY A MOMENT LONGER!
EEP.

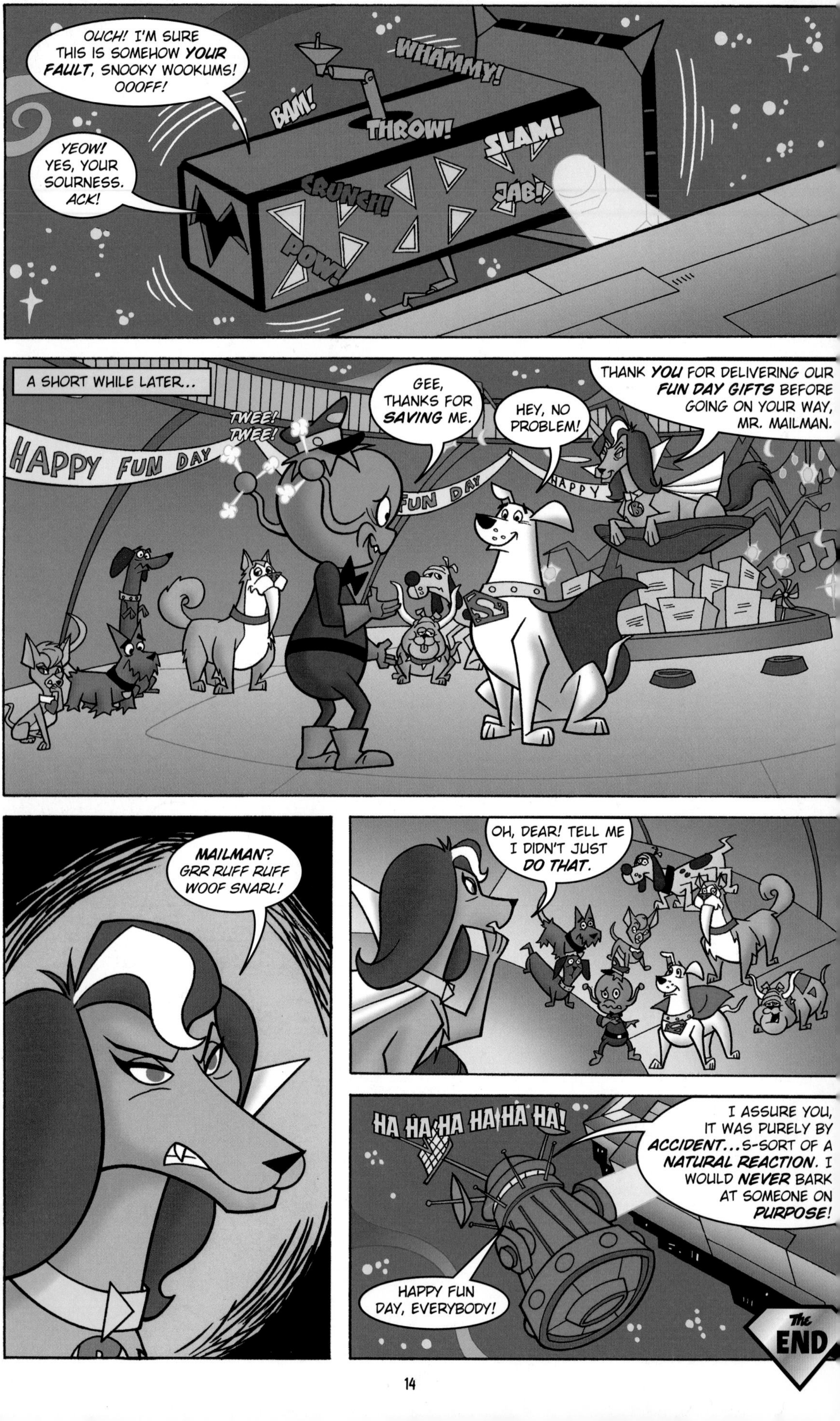
OUCH! I'M SURE THIS IS SOMEHOW YOUR FAULT, SNOOKY WOOKUMS! OOOFF!
WHAMMY!
BAM!
THROW!
SLAM!
YEOW! YES, YOUR SOURNESS. ACK!
CRUNCH!
JAB!
POW!
A SHORT WHILE LATER...
TWEE! TWEE!
HAPPY FUN DAY
GEE, THANKS FOR SAVING ME.
HEY, NO PROBLEM!
THANK YOU FOR DELIVERING OUR FUN DAY GIFTS BEFORE GOING ON YOUR WAY, MR. MAILMAN.
FUN DAY
HAPPY
MAILMAN? GRR RUFF RUFF WOOF SNARL!
OH, DEAR! TELL ME I DIDN'T JUST DO THAT.
HA HA HA HA HA HA!
I ASSURE YOU, IT WAS PURELY BY ACCIDENT...S-SORT OF A NATURAL REACTION. I WOULD NEVER BARK AT SOMEONE ON PURPOSE!
HAPPY FUN DAY, EVERYBODY!
The END

YOU BET YOUR SWEET BEPPO!

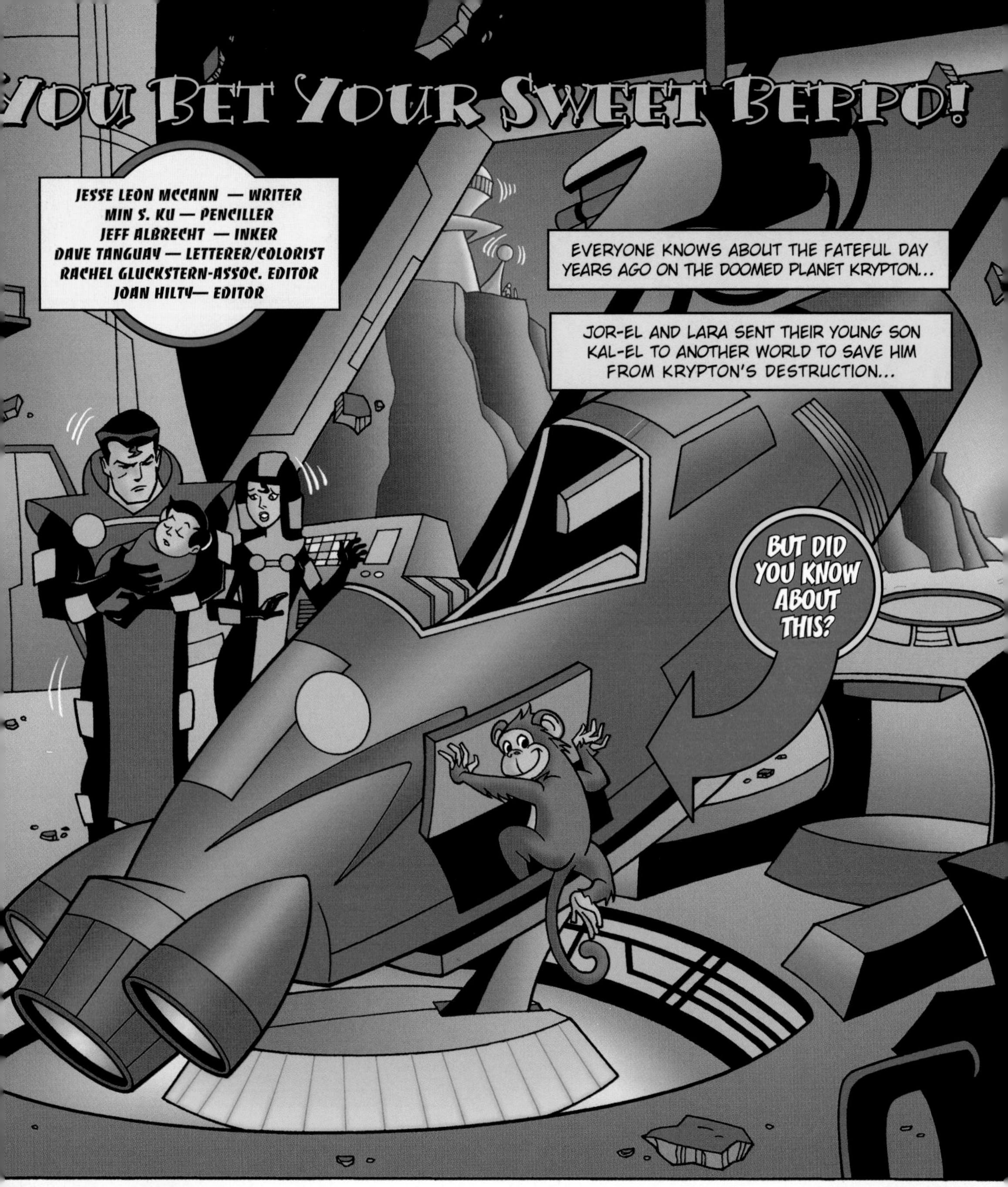
JESSE LEON McCANN — WRITER
MIN S. KU — PENCILLER
JEFF ALBRECHT — INKER
DAVE TANGUAY — LETTERER/COLORIST
RACHEL GLUCKSTERN-ASSOC. EDITOR
JOAN HILTY— EDITOR
EVERYONE KNOWS ABOUT THE FATEFUL DAY YEARS AGO ON THE DOOMED PLANET KRYPTON...
JOR-EL AND LARA SENT THEIR YOUNG SON KAL-EL TO ANOTHER WORLD TO SAVE HIM FROM KRYPTON'S DESTRUCTION...
BUT DID YOU KNOW ABOUT THIS?

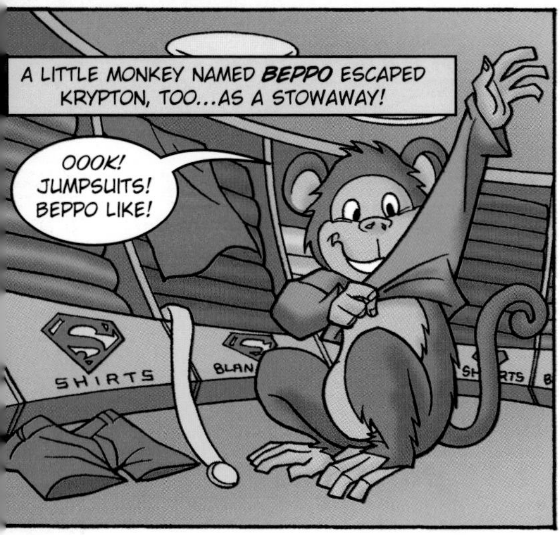
A LITTLE MONKEY NAMED *BEPPO* ESCAPED KRYPTON, TOO...AS A STOWAWAY!
OOOK! JUMPSUITS! BEPPO LIKE!
SHIRTS

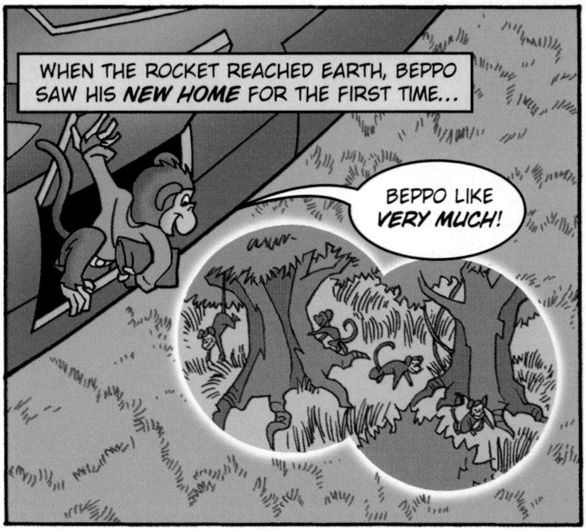
WHEN THE ROCKET REACHED EARTH, BEPPO SAW HIS *NEW HOME* FOR THE FIRST TIME...
BEPPO LIKE *VERY MUCH!*

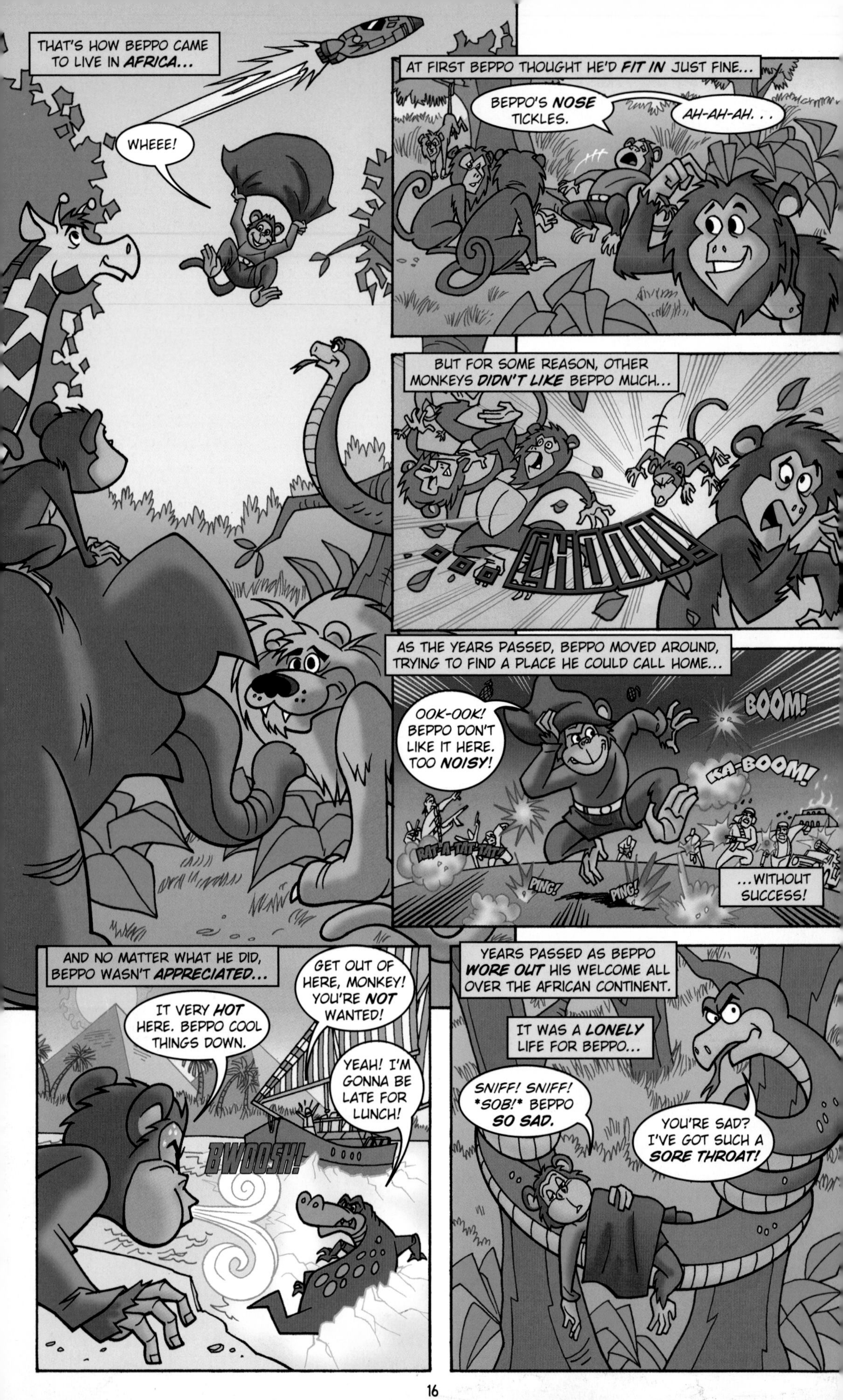
THAT'S HOW BEPPO CAME TO LIVE IN AFRICA...
WHEEE!
AT FIRST BEPPO THOUGHT HE'D FIT IN JUST FINE...
BEPPO'S NOSE TICKLES.
AH-AH-AH. . .
BUT FOR SOME REASON, OTHER MONKEYS DIDN'T LIKE BEPPO MUCH...
CHOOO!
AS THE YEARS PASSED, BEPPO MOVED AROUND, TRYING TO FIND A PLACE HE COULD CALL HOME...
OOK-OOK! BEPPO DON'T LIKE IT HERE. TOO NOISY!
BOOM!
KA-BOOM!
RAT-A-TAT-TAT!
PING!
PING!
...WITHOUT SUCCESS!
AND NO MATTER WHAT HE DID, BEPPO WASN'T APPRECIATED...
IT VERY HOT HERE. BEPPO COOL THINGS DOWN.
GET OUT OF HERE, MONKEY! YOU'RE NOT WANTED!
YEAH! I'M GONNA BE LATE FOR LUNCH!
BWOOSH!
YEARS PASSED AS BEPPO WORE OUT HIS WELCOME ALL OVER THE AFRICAN CONTINENT.
IT WAS A LONELY LIFE FOR BEPPO...
SNIFF! SNIFF! *SOB!* BEPPO SO SAD.
YOU'RE SAD? I'VE GOT SUCH A SORE THROAT!

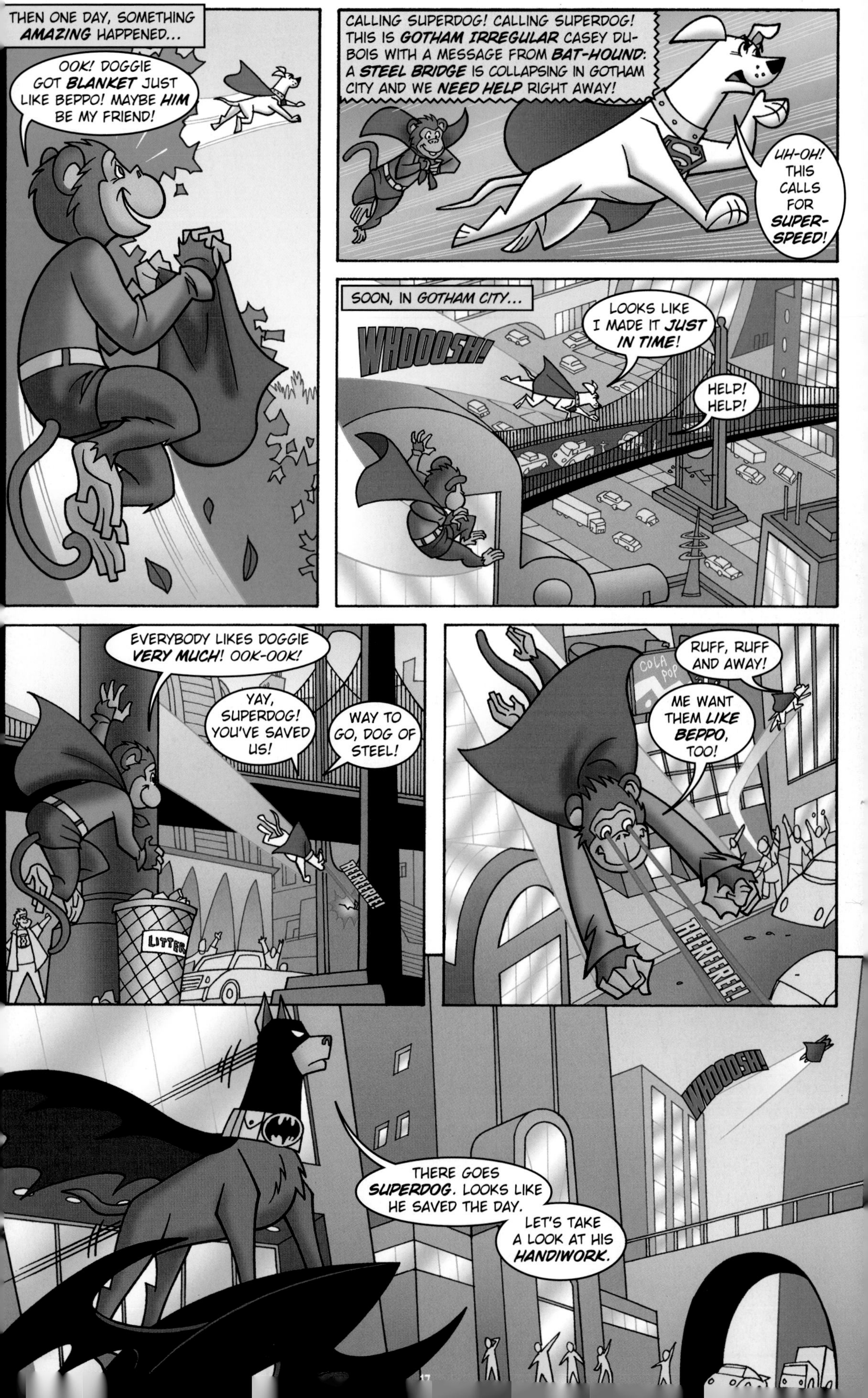
THEN ONE DAY, SOMETHING AMAZING HAPPENED...
OOK! DOGGIE GOT BLANKET JUST LIKE BEPPO! MAYBE HIM BE MY FRIEND!
CALLING SUPERDOG! CALLING SUPERDOG! THIS IS GOTHAM IRREGULAR CASEY DUBOIS WITH A MESSAGE FROM BAT-HOUND: A STEEL BRIDGE IS COLLAPSING IN GOTHAM CITY AND WE NEED HELP RIGHT AWAY!
UH-OH! THIS CALLS FOR SUPER-SPEED!
SOON, IN GOTHAM CITY...
WHOOOSH!
LOOKS LIKE I MADE IT JUST IN TIME!
HELP! HELP!
EVERYBODY LIKES DOGGIE VERY MUCH! OOK-OOK!
YAY, SUPERDOG! YOU'VE SAVED US!
WAY TO GO, DOG OF STEEL!
REEREEREE!
LITTER
RUFF, RUFF AND AWAY!
ME WANT THEM LIKE BEPPO, TOO!
COLA POP
REEREEREE!
WHOOOSH!
THERE GOES SUPERDOG. LOOKS LIKE HE SAVED THE DAY.
LET'S TAKE A LOOK AT HIS HANDIWORK.

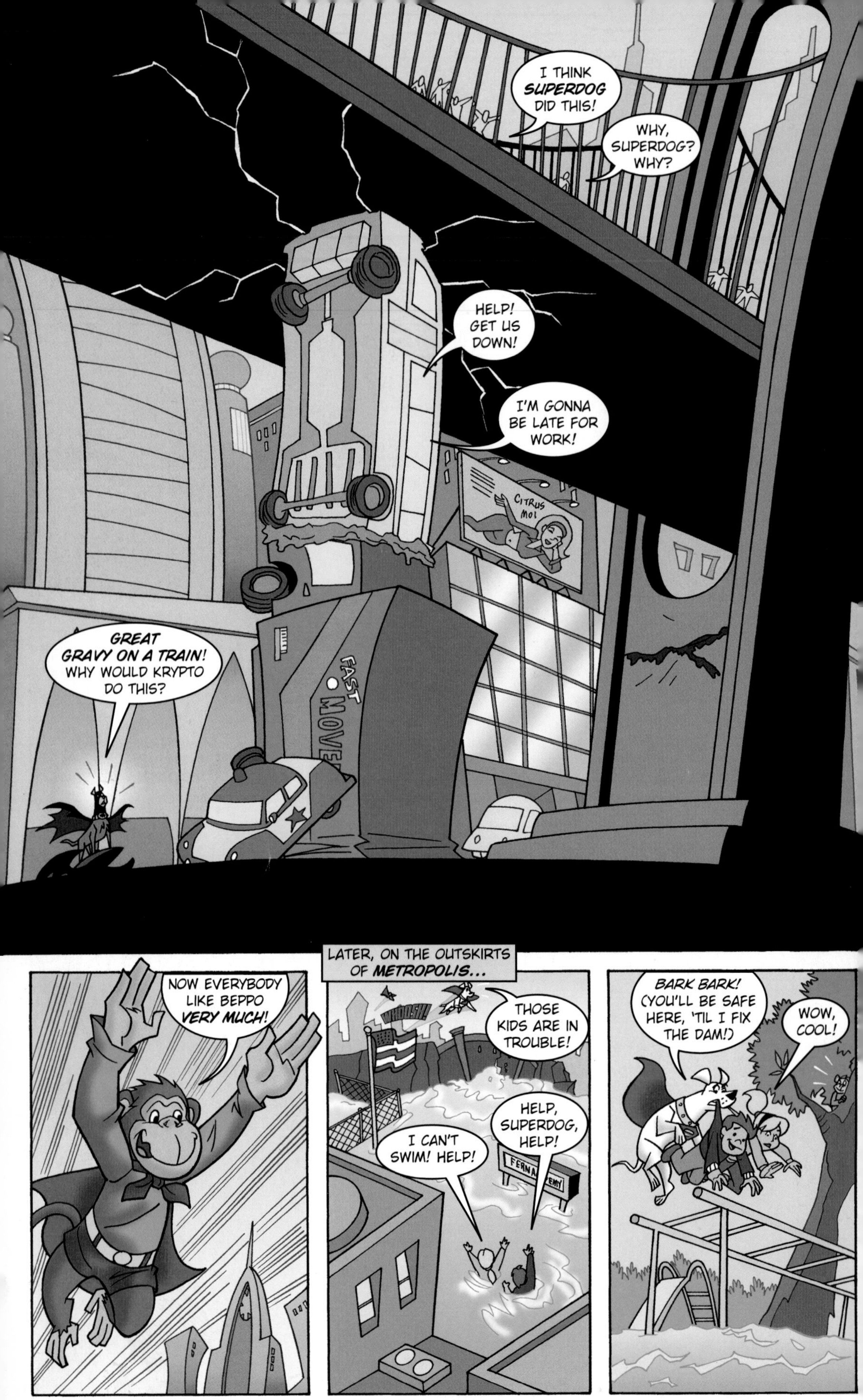

I THINK SUPERDOG DID THIS!
WHY, SUPERDOG? WHY?
HELP! GET US DOWN!
I'M GONNA BE LATE FOR WORK!
CITRUS MOI
GREAT GRAVY ON A TRAIN! WHY WOULD KRYPTO DO THIS?
FAST MOVE
NOW EVERYBODY LIKE BEPPO VERY MUCH!
LATER, ON THE OUTSKIRTS OF METROPOLIS...
WHOOSH!
THOSE KIDS ARE IN TROUBLE!
HELP, SUPERDOG, HELP!
I CAN'T SWIM! HELP!
BARK BARK! (YOU'LL BE SAFE HERE, 'TIL I FIX THE DAM!)
WOW, COOL!

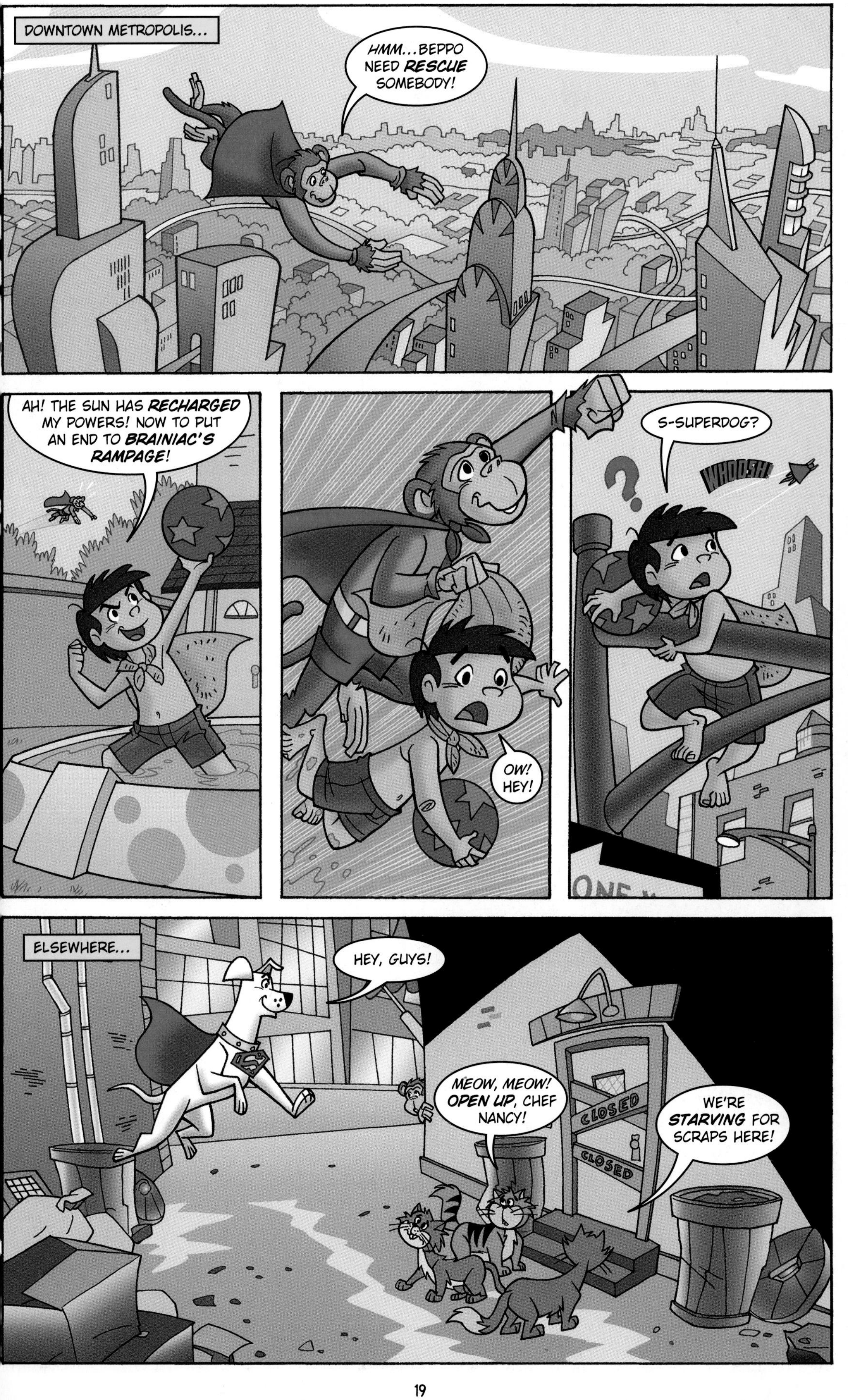
DOWNTOWN METROPOLIS...
HMM...BEPPO NEED RESCUE SOMEBODY!
AH! THE SUN HAS RECHARGED MY POWERS! NOW TO PUT AN END TO BRAINIAC'S RAMPAGE!
OW! HEY!
S-SUPERDOG?
WHOOSH!
ELSEWHERE...
HEY, GUYS!
MEOW, MEOW! OPEN UP, CHEF NANCY!
WE'RE STARVING FOR SCRAPS HERE!
CLOSED
CLOSED

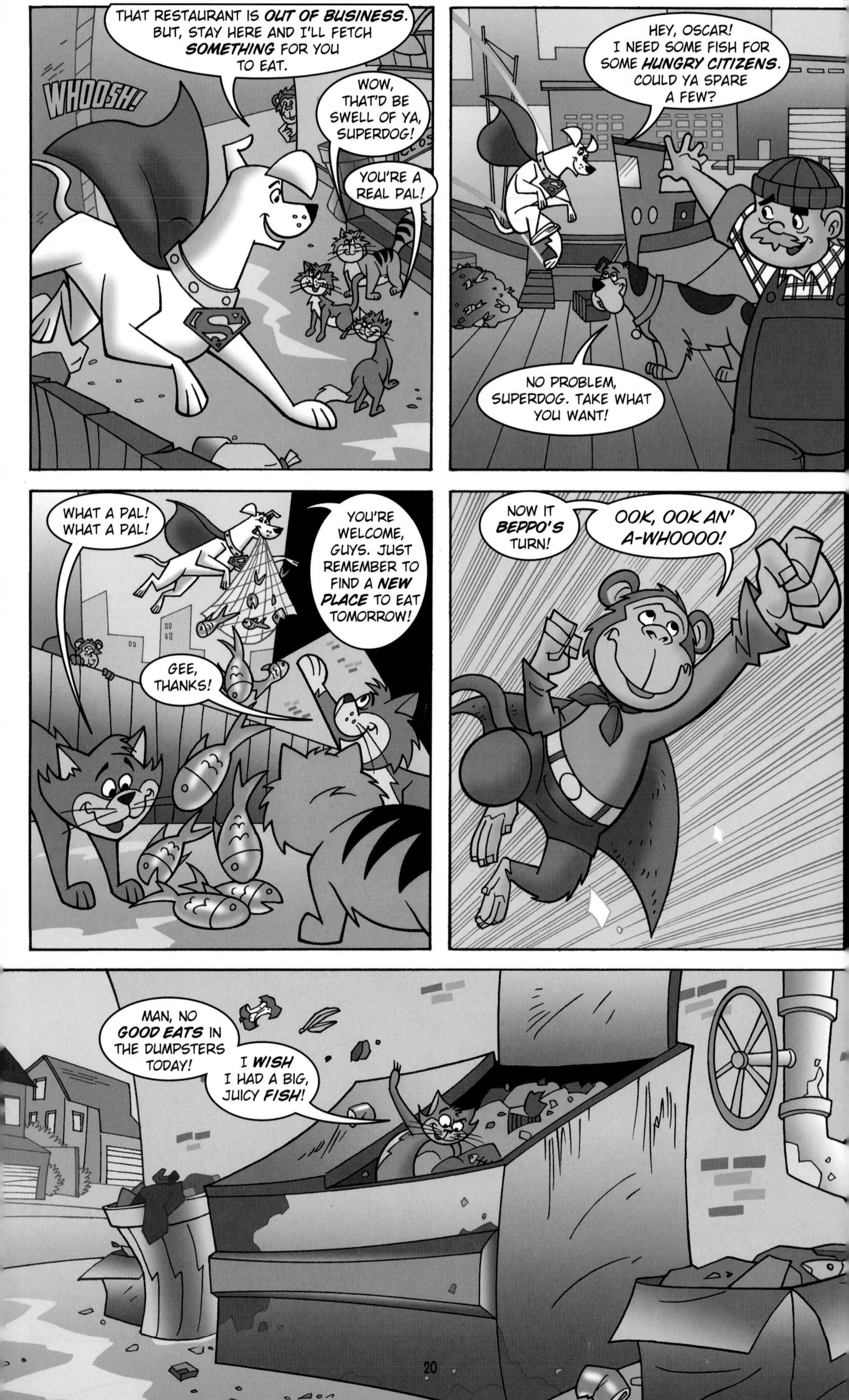

THAT RESTAURANT IS *OUT OF BUSINESS.* BUT, STAY HERE AND I'LL FETCH *SOMETHING* FOR YOU TO EAT.
WHOOSH!
WOW, THAT'D BE SWELL OF YA, SUPERDOG!
YOU'RE A REAL PAL!
HEY, OSCAR! I NEED SOME FISH FOR SOME *HUNGRY CITIZENS*. COULD YA SPARE A FEW?
NO PROBLEM, SUPERDOG. TAKE WHAT YOU WANT!
WHAT A PAL! WHAT A PAL!
YOU'RE WELCOME, GUYS. JUST REMEMBER TO FIND A *NEW PLACE* TO EAT TOMORROW!
GEE, THANKS!
NOW IT *BEPPO'S* TURN!
OOK, OOK AN' A-WHOOOO!
MAN, NO *GOOD EATS* IN THE DUMPSTERS TODAY!
I *WISH* I HAD A BIG, JUICY *FISH*!

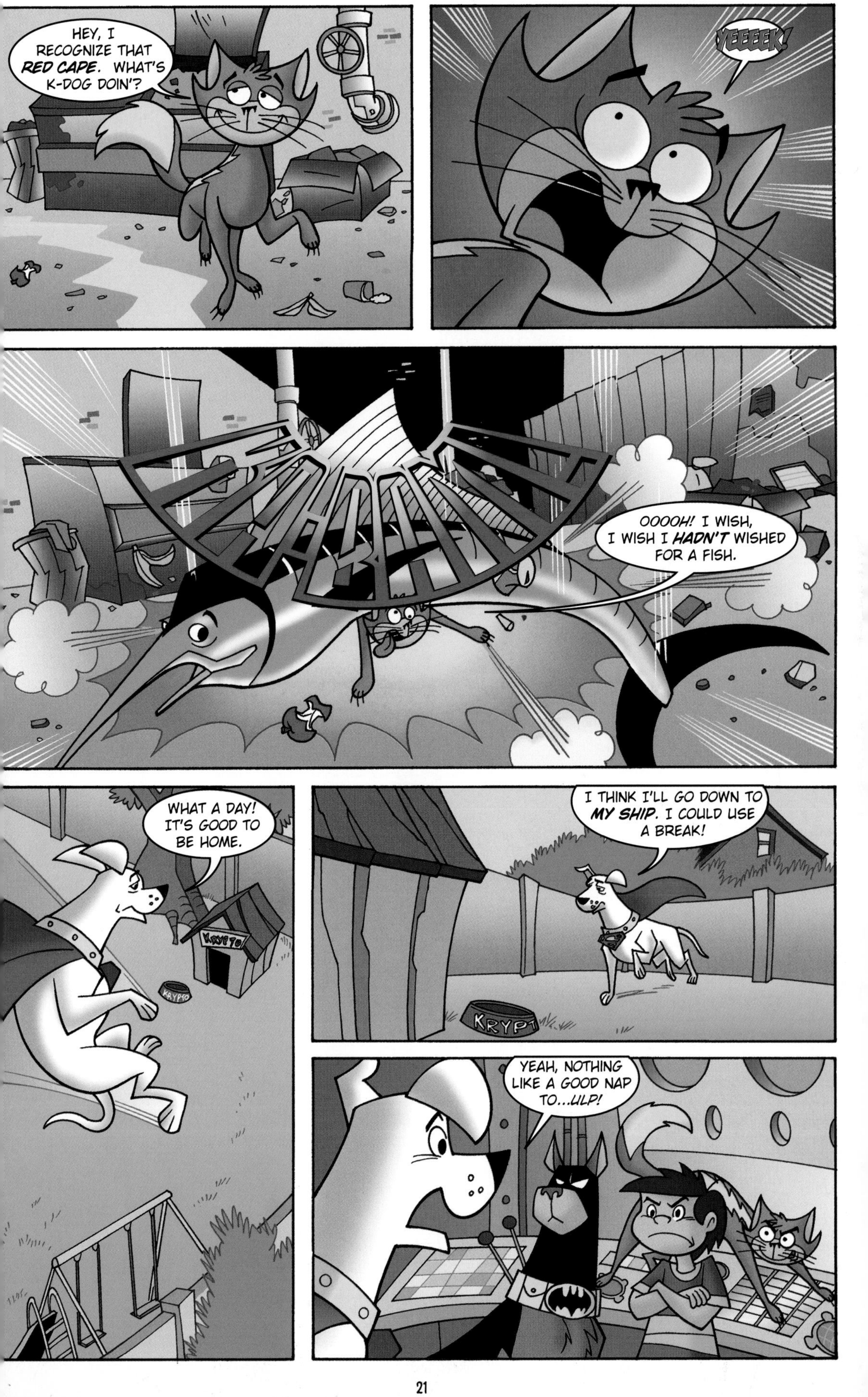
HEY, I RECOGNIZE THAT RED CAPE. WHAT'S K-DOG DOIN'?
YEEEEK!
OOOOH! I WISH, I WISH I HADN'T WISHED FOR A FISH.
WHAT A DAY! IT'S GOOD TO BE HOME.
KRYPTO
KRYPTO
I THINK I'LL GO DOWN TO MY SHIP. I COULD USE A BREAK!
KRYPT
YEAH, NOTHING LIKE A GOOD NAP TO...ULP!

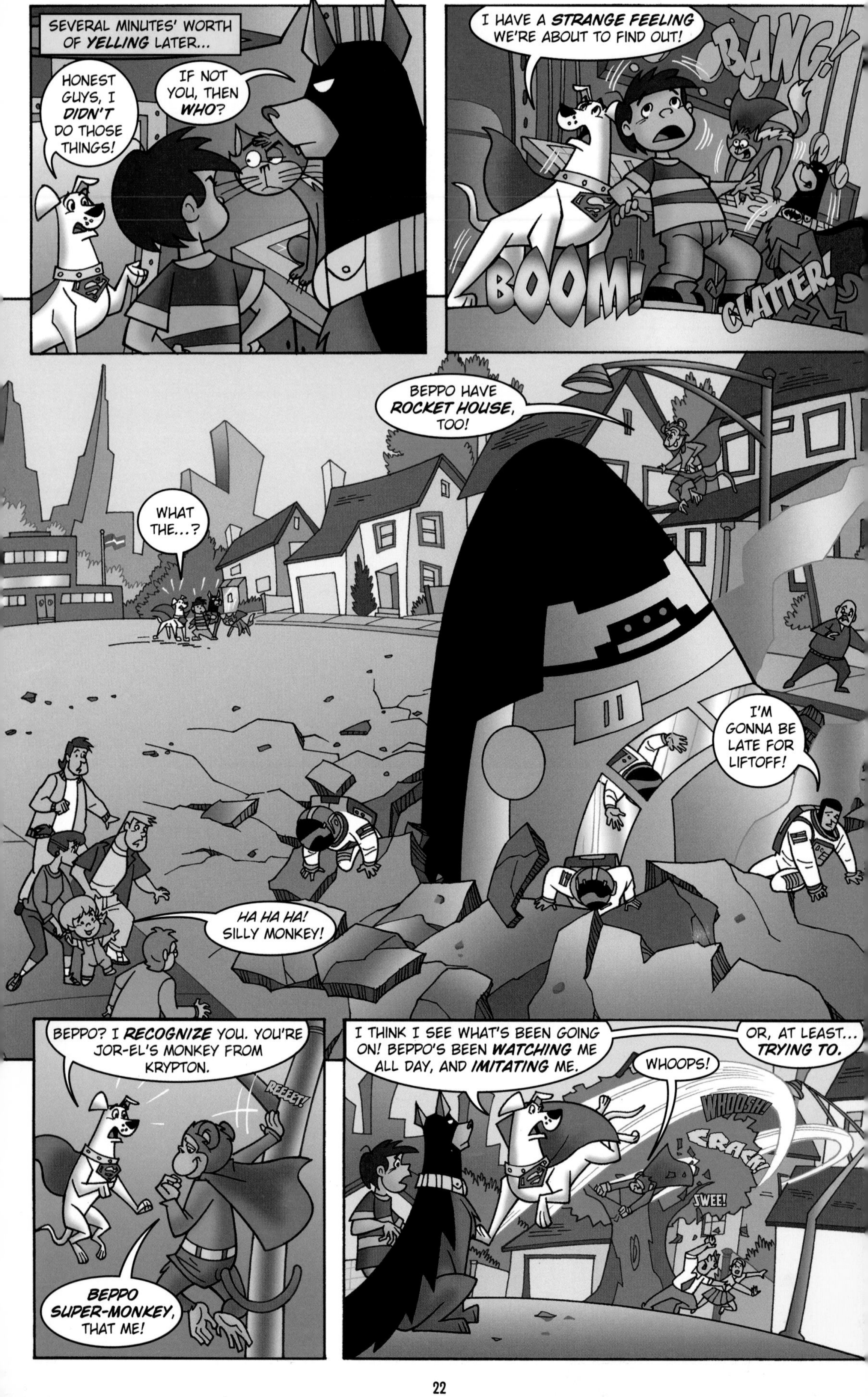
SEVERAL MINUTES' WORTH OF YELLING LATER...
HONEST GUYS, I DIDN'T DO THOSE THINGS!
IF NOT YOU, THEN WHO?
I HAVE A STRANGE FEELING WE'RE ABOUT TO FIND OUT!
BANG!
BOOM!
CLATTER!
BEPPO HAVE ROCKET HOUSE, TOO!
WHAT THE...?
I'M GONNA BE LATE FOR LIFTOFF!
HA HA HA! SILLY MONKEY!
BEPPO? I RECOGNIZE YOU. YOU'RE JOR-EL'S MONKEY FROM KRYPTON.
REEEEET!
BEPPO SUPER-MONKEY, THAT ME!
I THINK I SEE WHAT'S BEEN GOING ON! BEPPO'S BEEN WATCHING ME ALL DAY, AND IMITATING ME.
OR, AT LEAST... TRYING TO.
WHOOPS!
WHOOSH!
CRACK!
SWEE!

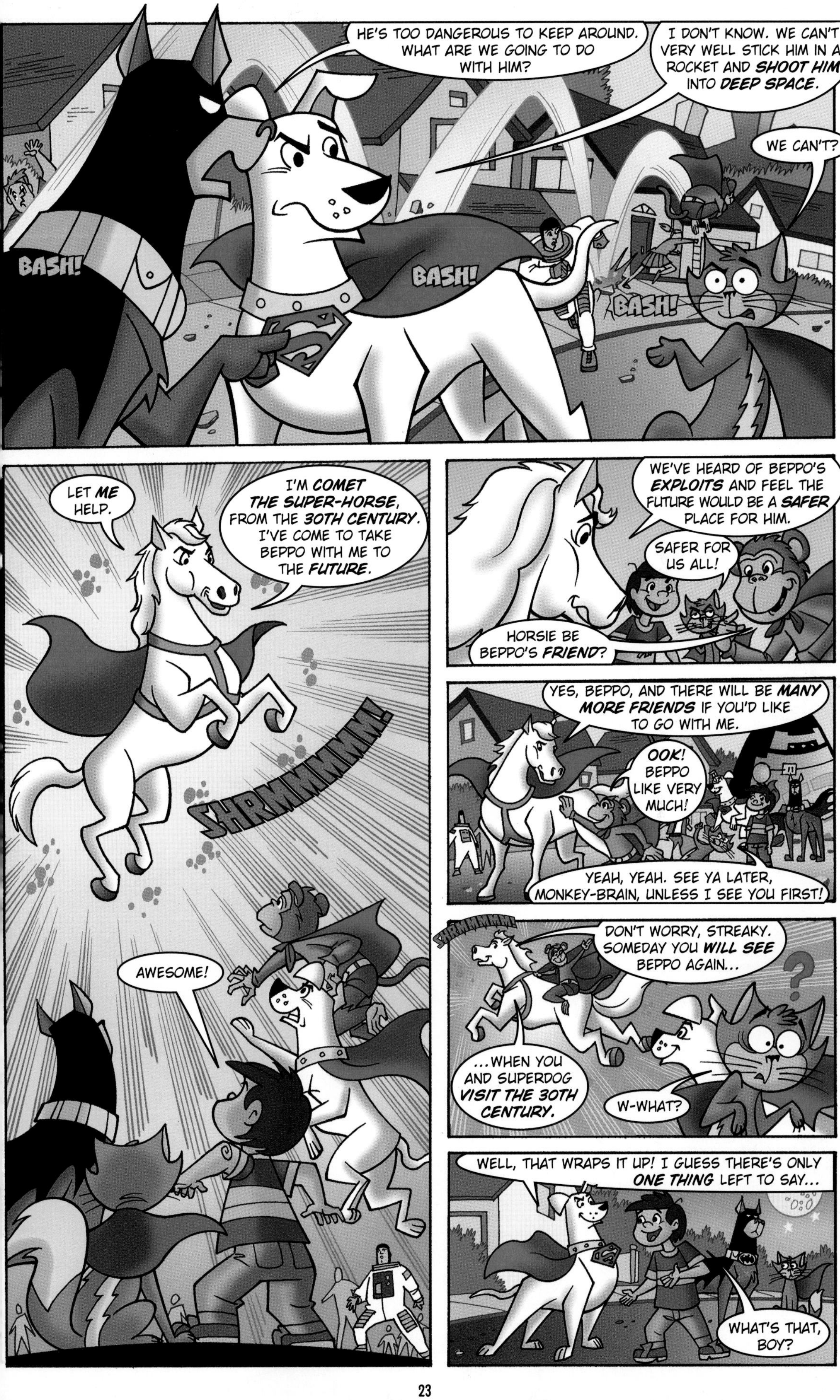
HE'S TOO DANGEROUS TO KEEP AROUND. WHAT ARE WE GOING TO DO WITH HIM?
I DON'T KNOW. WE CAN'T VERY WELL STICK HIM IN A ROCKET AND SHOOT HIM INTO DEEP SPACE.
WE CAN'T?
BASH!
BASH!
BASH!
LET ME HELP.
I'M COMET THE SUPER-HORSE, FROM THE 30TH CENTURY. I'VE COME TO TAKE BEPPO WITH ME TO THE FUTURE.
SHRMMMMM!
AWESOME!
WE'VE HEARD OF BEPPO'S EXPLOITS AND FEEL THE FUTURE WOULD BE A SAFER PLACE FOR HIM.
SAFER FOR US ALL!
HORSIE BE BEPPO'S FRIEND?
YES, BEPPO, AND THERE WILL BE MANY MORE FRIENDS IF YOU'D LIKE TO GO WITH ME.
OOK! BEPPO LIKE VERY MUCH!
YEAH, YEAH. SEE YA LATER, MONKEY-BRAIN, UNLESS I SEE YOU FIRST!
SHRMMMMM
DON'T WORRY, STREAKY. SOMEDAY YOU WILL SEE BEPPO AGAIN...
...WHEN YOU AND SUPERDOG VISIT THE 30TH CENTURY.
W-WHAT?
WELL, THAT WRAPS IT UP! I GUESS THERE'S ONLY ONE THING LEFT TO SAY...
WHAT'S THAT, BOY?

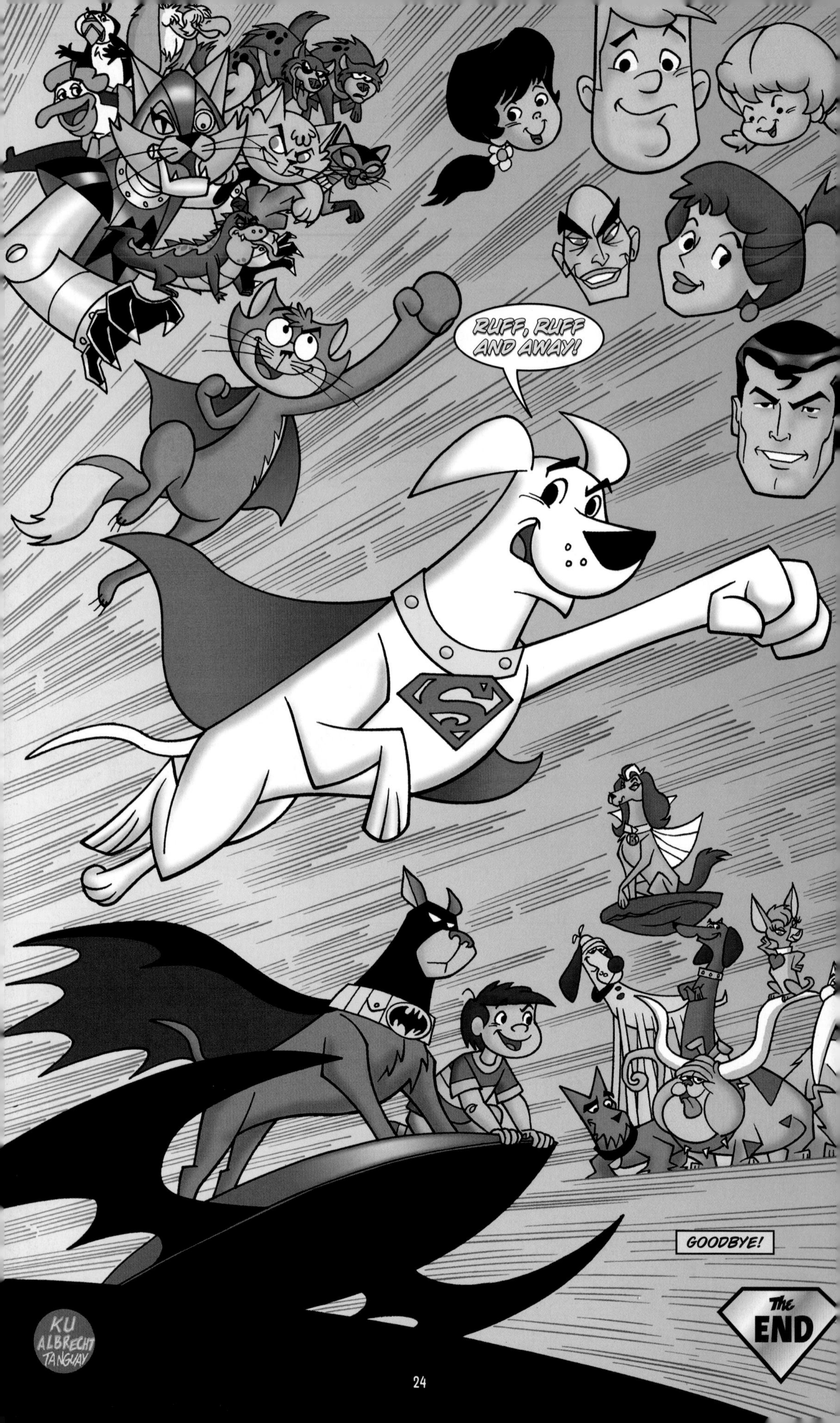
RUFF, RUFF AND AWAY!
GOODBYE!
The END
KU ALBRECHT TANGUAY

Superdog Jokes!

WHAT DO YOU CALL A DOG WHO HOSTS A LATE-NIGHT TALK SHOW?

CANINE O'BRIEN!

WHAT DO DOGS PLAYING VIDEO GAMES SAY WHEN THEY NEED A BREAK?

PRESS PAWS!

WHAT KIND OF DOG MAKES THE BEST VOLLEYBALL PLAYER?

A SETTER!

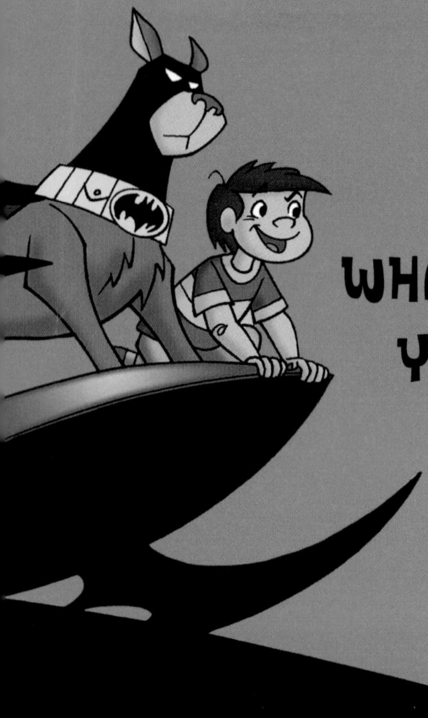

WHAT DO YOU CALL IT WHEN YOUR DOG RUNS AWAY?

A DOG-GONE DISASTER!

Creators

JESSE LEON MCCANN WRITER

Jesse Leon McCann is a *New York Times* Top-Ten Children's Book Writer, as well as a prolific all-ages comics writer. His credits include Pinky and the Brain, Animaniacs, and Looney Tunes for DC Comics; Scooby-Doo and Shrek 2 for Scholastic; and The Simpsons and Futurama for Bongo Comics. He lives in Los Angeles with his wife and four cats.

MIN SUNG KU PENCILLER

As a young child, Min Sung Ku dreamed of becoming a comic book illustrator. At six years old, he drew a picture of Superman standing behind the American flag. He has since achieved his childhood dream, having illustrated popular licensed comics properties like the Justice League, Batman Beyond, Spider-Man, Ben 10, Phineas & Ferb, the Replacements, the Proud Family, Krpyto the Superdog, and, of course, Superman. Min lives with his lovely wife and their beautiful twin daughters, Elisia and Eliana.

DAVE TANGUAY COLORIST/LETTERER

David Tanguay has over 20 years of experience in the comic book industry. He has worked as an editor, layout artist, colorist, and letterer. He has also done web design, and he taught computer graphics at the State University of New York.

Glossary

APPRECIATED (uh-PREE-shee-ate-id) — enjoyed or valued someone or something

CONTEMPTIBLE (kuhn-TEMPT-uh-buhl) — not worthy of respect

EXPLOITS (EK-sploitz) — brave and daring deeds

HANDIWORK (HAN-dee-wurk) — works or acts done by a specific person

HENCHMAN (HENCH-muhn) — a thug or criminal subordinate

IMITATING (IM-uh-tate-ing) — copying or mimicking someone or something

MARVELOUS (MAR-vuh-luhss) — very good or outstanding

RECOGNIZE (REK-uhg-nize) — to see someone or something and know who the person or thing is

UNINHABITED (uhn-in-HAB-uh-tid) — unoccupied or deserted

Visual Questions & Prompts

1. BASED ON WHAT YOU KNOW ABOUT BEPPO, WHY CAN WE SEE THROUGH THE TREES IN THIS PANEL?

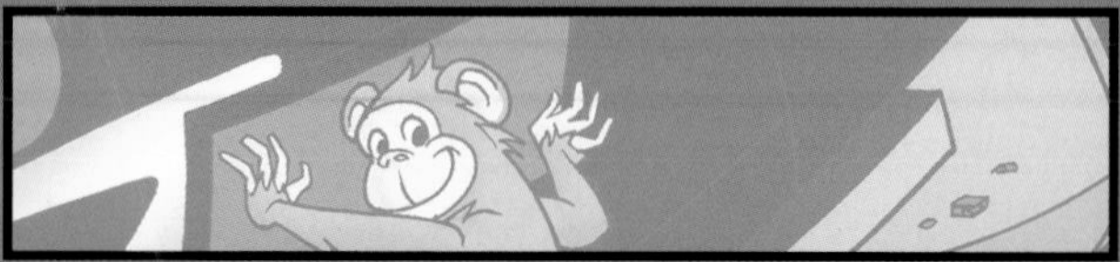

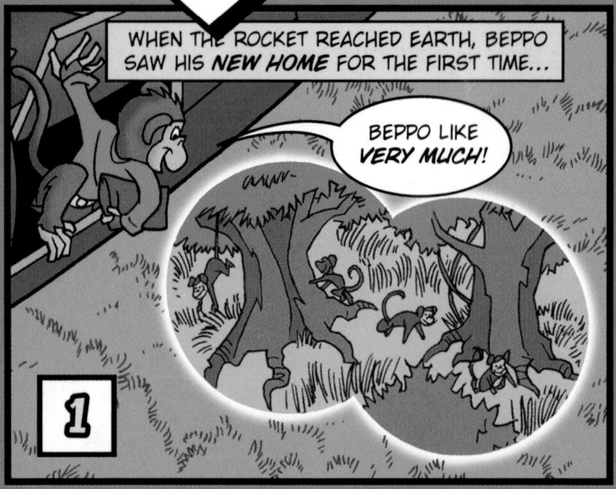
WHEN THE ROCKET REACHED EARTH, BEPPO SAW HIS *NEW HOME* FOR THE FIRST TIME...
BEPPO LIKE *VERY MUCH*!
1

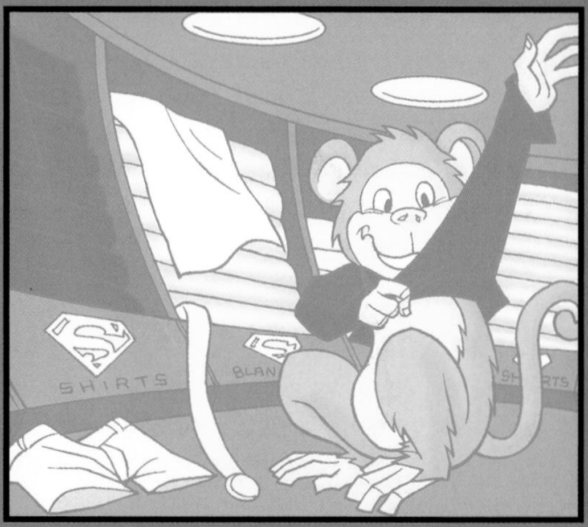
SHIRTS

2. OF ALL THE SUPER-PET SUPERPOWERS THAT ARE USED IN THIS BOOK, WHICH PET'S POWER DO YOU THINK IS THE COOLEST?

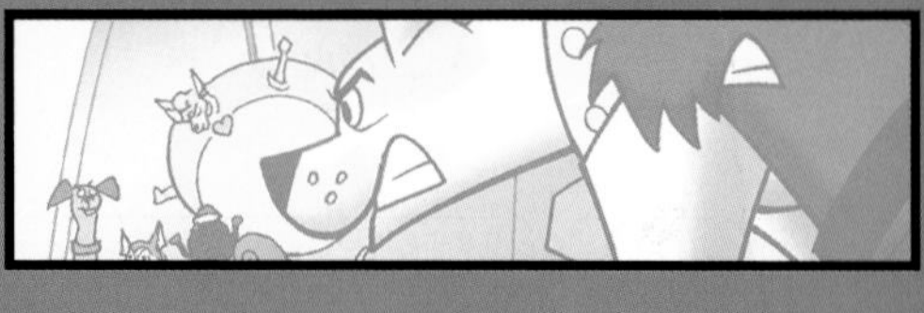

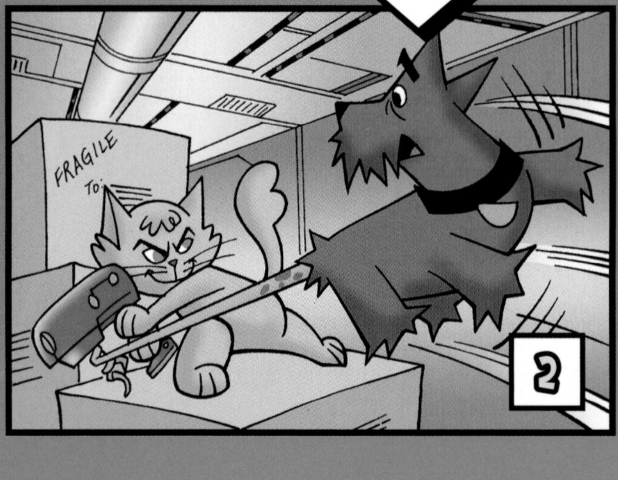
FRAGILE
To:
2

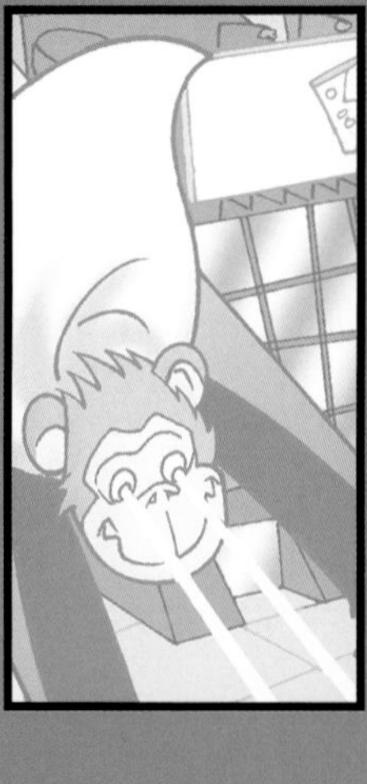

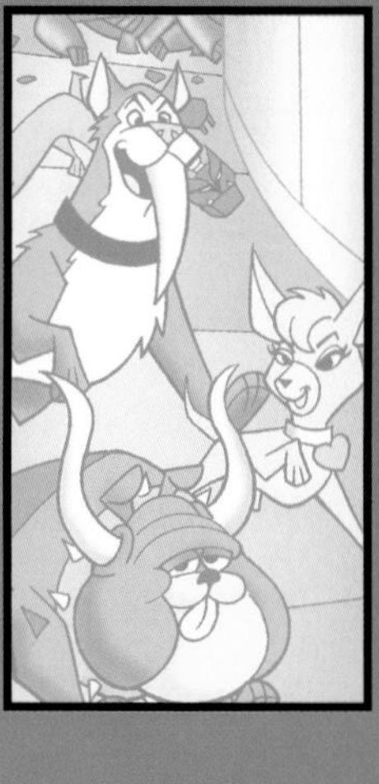

3. WHY DO YOU THINK THE ARTISTS CHOSE TO ADD BRIGHT LINES BEHIND COMET IN THIS PANEL?

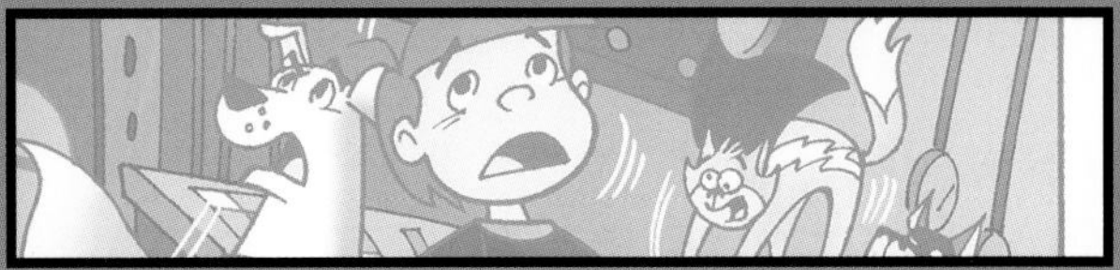

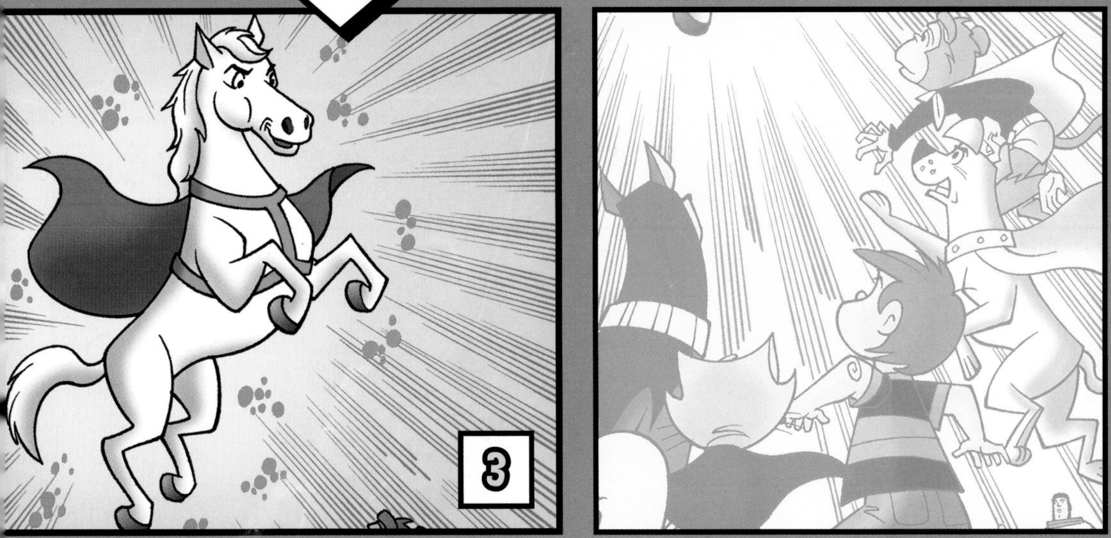
3

4. WHY DID BEPPO STRAND THIS BOY ON TOP OF A TELEPHONE POLE? WHAT WAS HE INTENDING TO DO, AND WHY DID HE MAKE A MISTAKE?

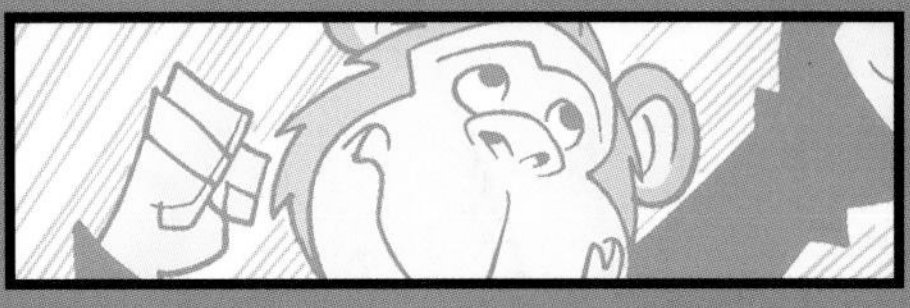

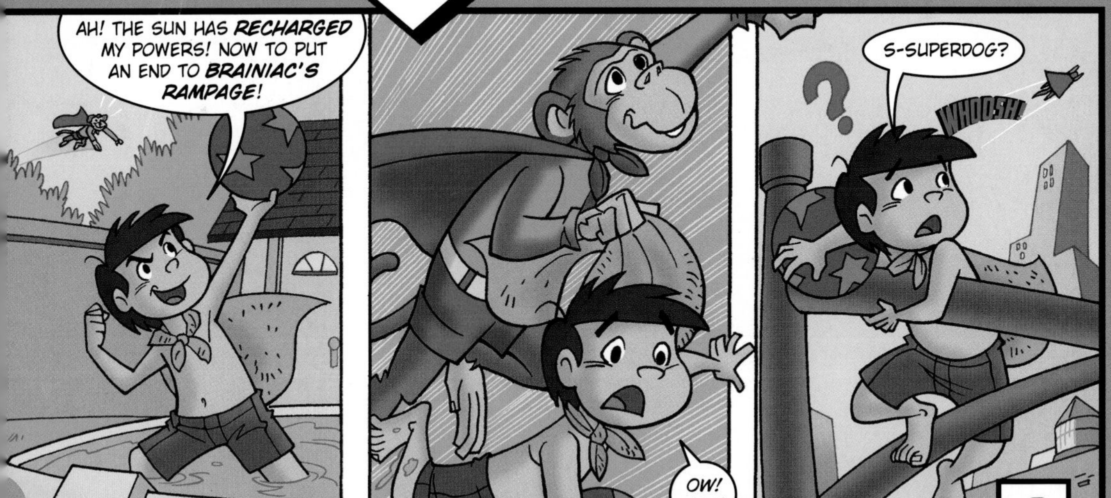
AH! THE SUN HAS *RECHARGED* MY POWERS! NOW TO PUT AN END TO *BRAINIAC'S RAMPAGE*!
OW! HEY!
S-SUPERDOG?
WHOOSH!
4

READ THEM ALL!

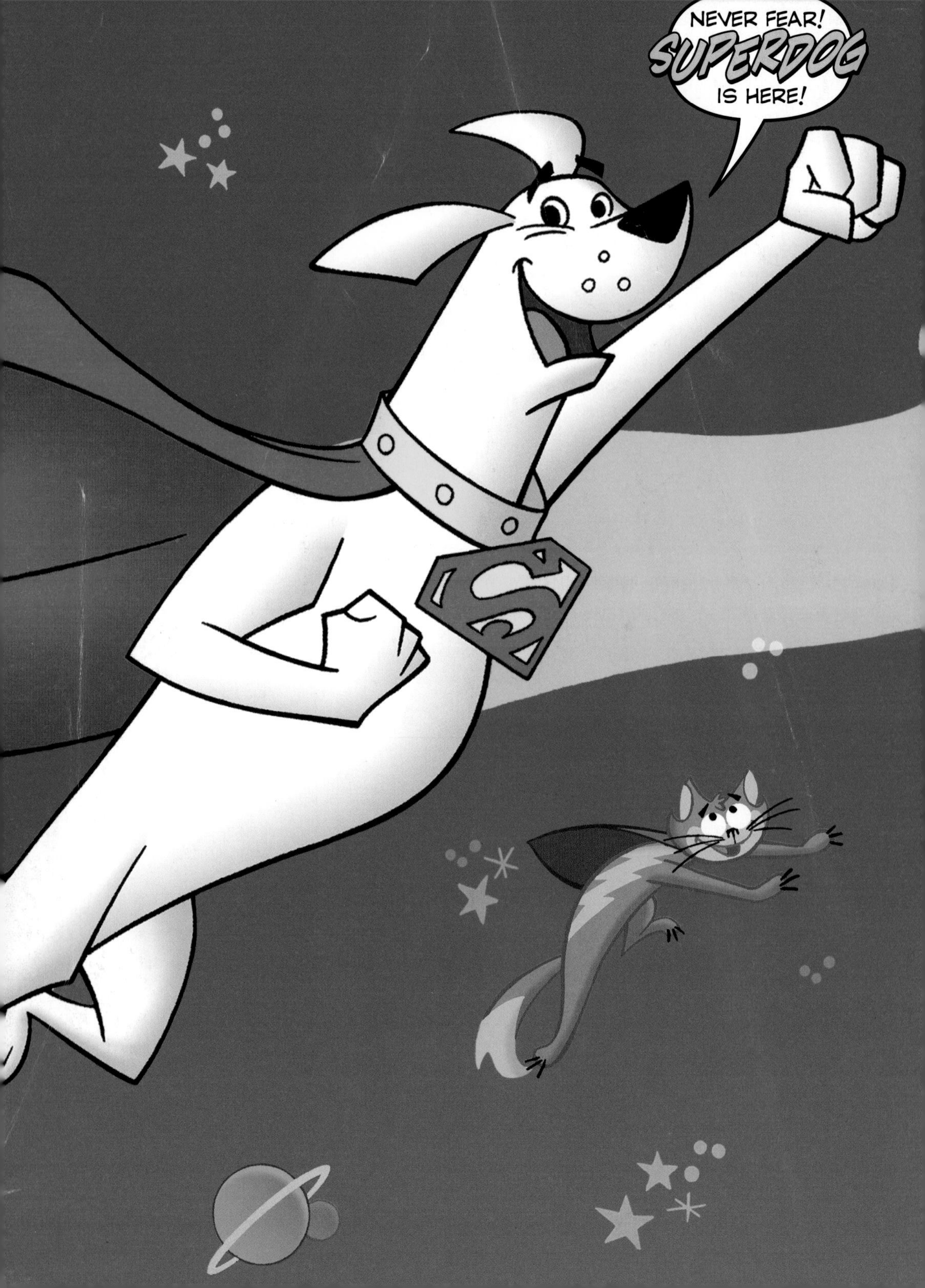
NEVER FEAR! SUPERDOG IS HERE!

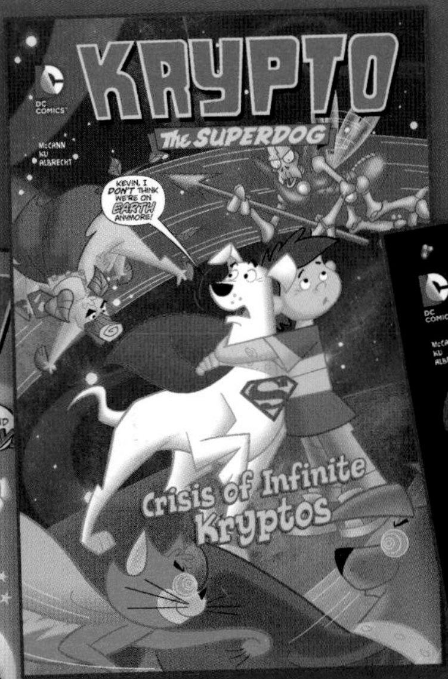
DC COMICS
KRYPTO
The SUPERDOG
McCANN
KU
ALBRECHT
KEVIN, I DON'T THINK WE'RE ON EARTH ANYMORE!
Crisis of Infinite Kryptos

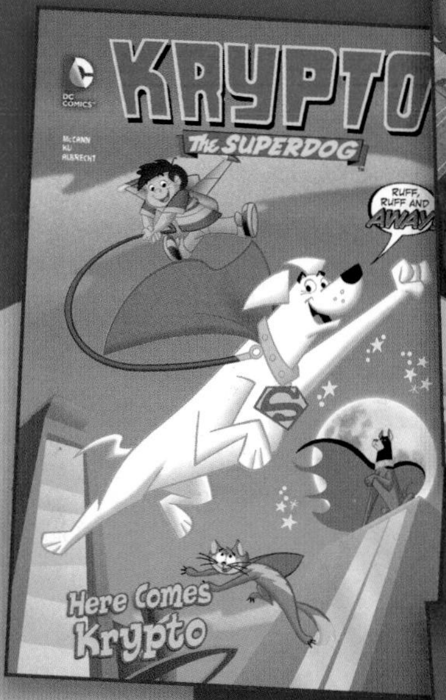
DC COMICS
KRYPTO
The SUPERDOG
McCANN
KU
ALBRECHT
RUFF, RUFF AND AWAY!
Here Comes Krypto

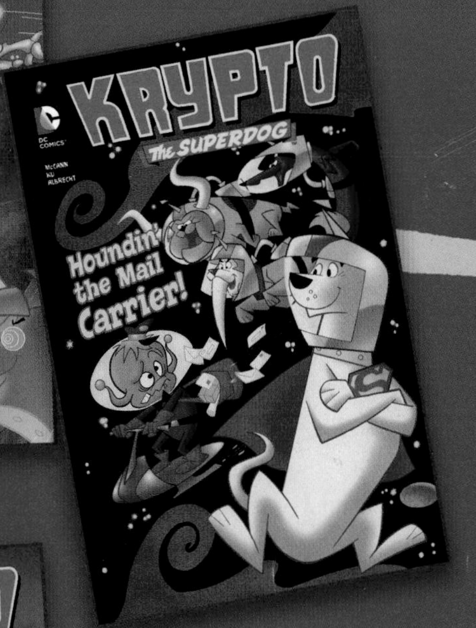
DC COMICS
KRYPTO
The SUPERDOG
McCANN
KU
ALBRECHT
Houndin' the Mail Carrier!

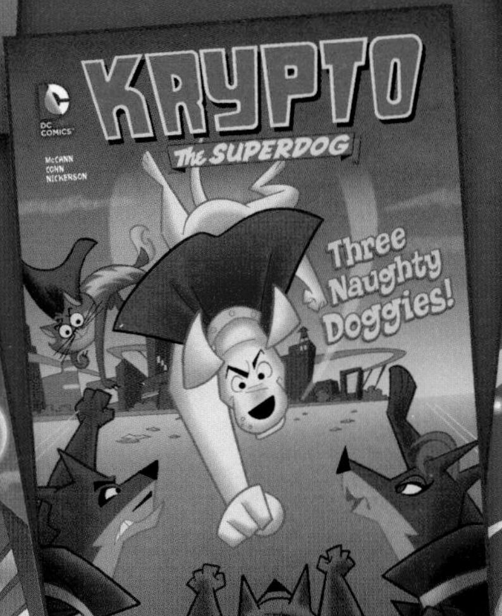
DC COMICS
KRYPTO
The SUPERDOG
McCANN
CONN
NICKERSON
Three Naughty Doggies!

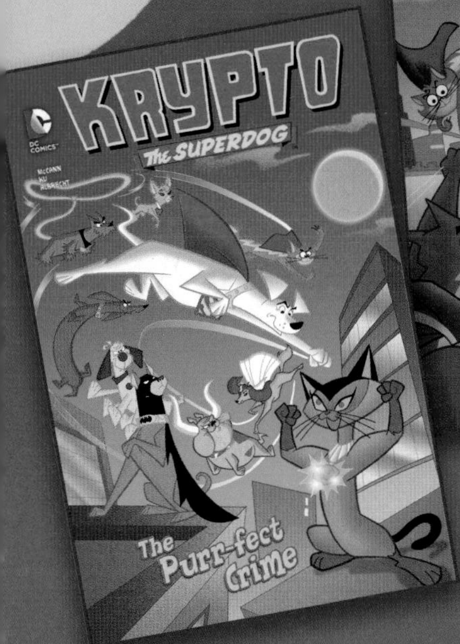
DC COMICS
KRYPTO
The SUPERDOG
McCANN
KU
ALBRECHT
The Purr-fect Crime

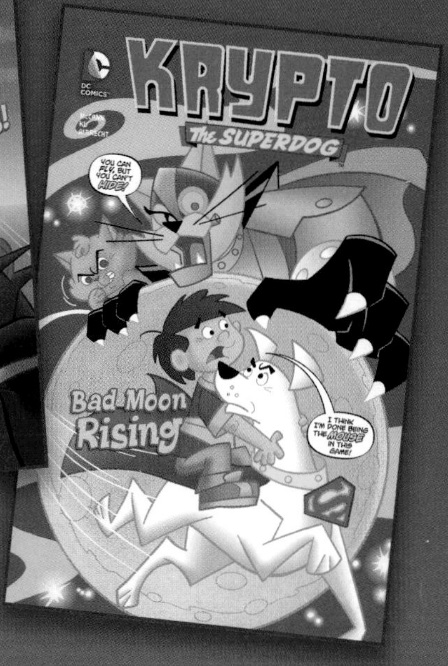
DC COMICS
KRYPTO
The SUPERDOG
YOU CAN FLY, BUT YOU CAN'T HIDE!
Bad Moon Rising
I THINK I'M DONE BEING THE MOUSE IN THIS GAME!

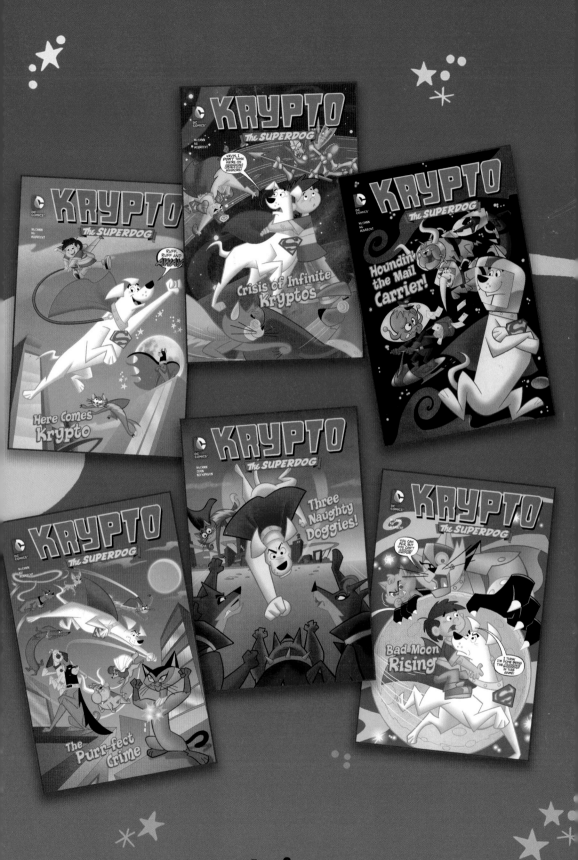

KRYPTO
The SUPERDOG™

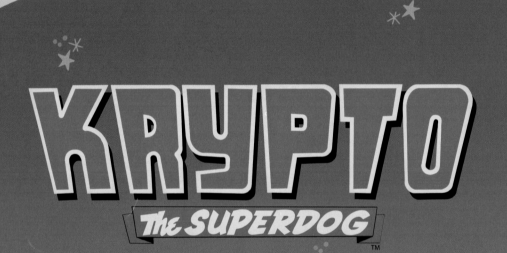